FAR EASTERN PROMISE

Lauren Adams knew that her life would change dramatically when she went to work for a British newspaper in Hong Kong. But could she really have fallen in love with her editor, David Kent, or was it just the romantic atmosphere of the island toying with her emotions? Before she learned the truth, she would be wined and dined by the Far East's biggest movie star and make an epic journey across mainland China.

JANET WHITEHEAD

◆

FAR EASTERN PROMISE

Complete and Unabridged

LINFORD
Leicester

First published in Great Britain in 1993 by
Robert Hale Limited
London

First Linford Edition
published 1998
by arrangement with
Robert Hale Limited
London

The right of Janet Whitehead to be identified
as the author of this work has been asserted
by her in accordance with the
Copyright, Designs and Patents Act, 1988

British Library CIP Data

Whitehead, Janet
    Far eastern promise.—Large print ed.—
Linford romance library
1. Love stories
2. Large type books
I. Title
823.9'14 [F]

ISBN 0–7089–5308–5

Published by
F. A. Thorpe (Publishing) Ltd.
Anstey, Leicestershire

Set by Words & Graphics Ltd.
Anstey, Leicestershire
Printed and bound in Great Britain by
T. J. International Ltd., Padstow, Cornwall

This book is printed on acid-free paper

This one is for the Tatlers —
Irene, Paul, Nicola,
Jonathan and Kimberley

1

Kai Tak Airport in Hong Kong is one of the most impressive airports in the world.

The runway extends straight out into Kowloon Bay. To reach it, planes have to swoop low over the high-rise buildings that stud the peninsula, and land swiftly and without error. On average, one plane sets down at Kai Tak every two and a half minutes, and unless this tricky manoeuvre is performed without mishap, the six or so 747s constantly circling overhead, patiently awaiting their own turn to land, would be up there all day.

Lauren Adams enjoyed the faint prospect of danger that accompanied any such landing, and when she saw Hong Kong float into view through the small, square window to her left, the exhaustion of the flight slipped quickly away from her to be replaced by a keen sense of anticipation, for her future lay here, or so she hoped. In Hong Kong she would realise her greatest dreams.

Yes, it had been a long haul from London, with stop-overs at Ankara, Kuwait, Bahrain, Dubai and Bangkok to ease the rigours of travel. But she was here at last; all the discomfort had been worth it.

Her plane gave a small, unpleasant lurch as it began its descent, but Lauren only felt her sense of expectancy rise. She was only minutes away from setting foot on Kowloon now, and then Hong Kong Island itself, and she could hardly wait.

She was a tall, lithe-limbed girl in her middle-twenties, with shoulder-length, dark-blonde hair and clear, well-spaced, inquisitive blue eyes. Now, as the plane dipped still lower, a brief, eager smile touched her full, pale pink lips. She had waited a long time for this moment. The opportunity of a lifetime awaited her down there, in that sprawling metropolis, and she intended to seize it hungrily, with both hands.

It had always been Lauren's desire to be a journalist, and from secondary school onwards she had worked single-mindedly to achieve that goal. She was naturally inquisitive and possessed of a direct manner. She was ambitious, not afraid to speak her mind or ask questions, and had a desire for truth and knowledge. She was also a very talented writer.

But these attributes alone were no guarantee of a job, as she soon learned after leaving college with a degree in journalism. The hey-day of Fleet Street was gone. Few of the big national dailies were willing to take a chance on an untried newcomer. They advised her to learn her craft, really *learn* it, on one of the provincial papers, and because she was so determined to succeed she went and did exactly that, finding a job first with one of the free-sheets distributed in her home county of Essex, and later on one of the more prestigious local papers.

But if Lauren had one fault, it was her ambition. It was a fearsome thing, and it drove her without mercy. Covering council meetings, fetes and jumble sales was all well and good for those who were content to plod along without initiative, but she wanted — needed — more of a challenge. So she went back to the big dailies, but they said she still had a lot to learn, and she was too stubborn to come right out and admit that they were right.

It had been a very frustrating period of her life, and she had grown increasingly restless and despondent. On the one hand she knew that she must put in her apprenticeship just like everyone else. But on the other, she knew that she had learned everything the provincials were likely to teach her.

It seemed that she had become the victim of a vicious circle. But then she had seen the advert which was to change her life. A small newspaper based in Hong Kong, published specifically for the English-speaking community there and aptly called *The Ex-Pat*, was looking for a features writer. The successful candidate would be given a six-month trial. After that, if both parties were agreeable, the position would be made permanent.

Lauren had applied for the post without hesitation. She had picked up a reasonable working grasp of Chinese from a room-mate at college, and had always enjoyed travel. Her parents had instilled in her a strong streak of independence, and the idea of going to work abroad did not so much daunt her as offer a much-needed challenge.

In time she had forgotten all about the application, and thought no more about it until a letter arrived at her digs one day asking her to attend an interview, which, as it transpired, went very well. She had been offered the job, had accepted, and now, with all the formalities behind her at long last, here she was.

Lauren felt a familiar surge of excitement. How she had dreamed of this moment whilst still living in London! At last her career was finally starting to blossom!

* * *

The plane touched down safely and within minutes a courtesy bus was ferrying the travellers across the tarmac to the terminal.

As soon as Lauren had left the almost-chilly airconditioning of the plane she realised she had been wise to wear only a thin, sky-blue cotton dress, for the weather was humid, this being July and the middle of the monsoon season. By the time the bus reached its destination, practically all of the new arrivals were using magazines, guidebooks or passports as makeshift fans.

The airport was bustling. Planes droned a constant accompaniment to all the hubbub, either just departing or just arriving. The terminal itself was a rather ugly building, but since it had been designed to handle more than twelve million passengers every year, the emphasis was on practicality rather than comfort. Furthermore, it seemed as if every one of those twelve million travellers were here today! Everywhere she looked, Lauren saw men, women and children of every age and nationality.

But there was an undeniable electricity in the air, that indefinable excitement that only exists at airports, and as Lauren shifted her shoulder-bag to a more comfortable position, she began to soak up the atmosphere, already composing in her mind the letter she would write to her parents tonight, a letter that would in some way try to convey the pleasure of this moment.

She made her way to immigration, and from there to customs and then baggage check. The airport officials were thorough in their search of her belongings, but since she had nothing to declare and even less to hide, she was soon wheeling her cases out into the buffer hall.

There seemed to be even more people congregated here, most of them holding up signs upon which had been written the names of the travellers they were hoping to meet.

Although Lauren (who was as self-reliant as she was ambitious) had told her new employer that she could find her own way to his office upon her arrival, he had insisted that someone would be at Kai Tak to meet her, so now she paused in the great, echo-filled hall and began to scan the veritable forest of signs in search of her own name.

She finally spotted the sign she was looking for — though not the person holding it — on her second sweep, and began to push her baggage cart in that direction.

When she was near enough, she saw a tiny Oriental girl, possibly Lauren's own age or maybe a little younger.

The girl had her raven-black hair cut in a neat bob. It shone a deep blue in the overhead lights. She had large hazel eyes, a small button nose and a wide mouth. Her very slim figure was encased in a neat jade-green dress of typically-Chinese design, high at the throat, quite long and with neat little half-sleeves.

At first the girl did not see Lauren making her way towards her. Then at last she focused on the tall blonde girl in the smart but sensible sky-blue dress and a question formed itself clearly on her round face.

When Lauren was near enough, the little Chinese girl asked hesitantly, "Lau-ren? Lau-ren . . . Ad-ams?" She seemed relieved to have pronounced it correctly.

Lauren nodded, and when she spoke she did so slowly, so that she would not lose the other girl. "Yes, I'm Lauren Adams. And you must be . . . ?"

The Oriental girl stuck out her right hand and a broad, infectious grin spread across her face. "Maggie Cheung," she replied, continuing in quite acceptable English, "Mr David sent me. Pick you up."

David, she thought. That would be David Kent, the *Ex-Pat* editor, whom she had met at her interview a couple of months earlier, and as his name came into her mind, so too did a vivid recollection of the man himself; tall, athletic, with a rugged face tanned by the warm Oriental sun, and a square, well-defined jaw. Again she saw David Kent's eyes as he had appraised her across the desk in the *Ex-Pat*'s London office, remembered their dark brown twinkle, the merest hint of his wicked sense of humour in the line of his mouth, the thick black hair brushed carelessly back from his forehead; and recalling him now gave her the most curious feeling inside, an altogether different feeling of anticipation — anticipation at seeing him again.

"We go?" asked Maggie Cheung,

indicating one of the terminal's three exits.

Momentarily distracted by the memory of David Kent, Lauren had to take a moment to come back down to earth. "Go?" she repeated stupidly.

Maggie nodded, sending a shiver through her dark hair. "Go," she repeated. "Leave. Depart. Exit. Set off." And here her grin grew even wider. "Do a bunk."

Lauren studied her new acquaintance carefully. She wasn't sure if Maggie was being sarcastic or genuinely trying to explain herself further. Then the young Chinese girl went on quite proudly, "I have good English, yes?"

Lauren allowed herself to relax and smile. "Very good English," she replied. "All right, Maggie, I'm in your hands. Lead on."

The Chinese girl turned and hurried through the crowd, and Lauren had to push her baggage cart along swiftly just to keep up with her. Maggie led them to the left-hand exit and out into the

11

airport car-park. The sky was cloudless and there was no breeze to stir the trees or flags they passed on their way to the car in which the Oriental girl had driven out to meet her.

"Your flight, she was good?" Maggie asked over her shoulder.

"It was *long*," Lauren replied. "But at least there were no major delays."

"You must feel tired, yes?"

"To be honest with you, I think I'm too excited to feel tired," Lauren admitted ruefully.

They reached a small, silver-coloured Metro and Maggie unlocked the boot and set about helping her to transfer her luggage from the cart to the car. "Mr David, he is looking very forward to meeting you again," she remarked, and Lauren knew another surprising shiver of pleasure at the knowledge, though why she should feel that way about a man she hardly knew, she couldn't say. Indeed, it was in itself strange that she should find David Kent so appealing; until now, she had

12

displayed little real interest in *any* man — she had been too devoted to her career for that.

The luggage finally packed away, Lauren tipped a porter to return the cart to the airport and then climbed into the car beside Maggie. Within moments the Oriental girl was steering them out of the carpark.

"We will have to cross Kowloon Bay by way of the Cross-Harbour Tunnel," Maggie explained as she sent them whizzing along the expressway leading to Victoria Harbour. "But that is a shame. The Star Ferry would have given you a much nicer view of Hong Kong — but the ferry doesn't take cars."

Lauren was already getting a glimpse of the island from the passenger-side window of the car, however. In the foreground, the bay was a riot of activity. Green and white ferries ploughed steadily back and forth through the water, as did junks and sampans and motor-boats and tankers.

Then came the harbour-front, where a jumble of ultramodern skyscrapers shelved back from the blue, sun-dappled water, all of it set against a backdrop of deep green hills, until recently just pictures in a brochure, but now the real thing, and absolutely breathtaking because of it.

"You work at the *Ex-Pat*?" Lauren asked, glancing at her companion's profile.

Maggie nodded without taking her hazel eyes off the motorway. "*Shi*. Yes. Secret-ary. Typist. Telephone operator." She searched for the right expression and finally said, "Girl Wednesday."

Lauren smiled. "You mean 'Girl Friday'."

"No," Maggie replied seriously. "Only work on Wednesdays."

"Oh. You're a part-timer, then?"

The Oriental girl nodded. "I worked full-time when there was more to do. Now there is not so much as there once was."

Lauren felt a frown pucker her

14

brow, for that sounded ominous. The impression David Kent had given her at her interview was one of a progressive, successful newspaper — not one that switched its employees to part-time because there wasn't much work to do.

Before she could pursue the subject, however, Maggie said, "You are hungry?"

Until now, Lauren hadn't really thought about food, but she hadn't eaten much over the last couple of days — a combination of travel and excitement — and now that she had finally reached her destination, she *was* starting to feel hungry.

"Yes, I am a bit."

"I will prepare us something when we get home."

"Home?" Lauren echoed.

Maggie could not resist the opportunity to show off her command of the English language once again. "Home," she repeated, her grin revealing teeth like pearls. "Abode. Dwelling. Habitation. Residence."

"Yes, I know what 'home' means," Lauren replied, beginning to like this girl's company. "I was just querying exactly what you *meant* by the word. You made it sound as if it was home for the both of us."

The Oriental girl chanced a glance at her. "It is — as long as you do not mind sharing with me."

"Of course I don't. But — "

"Mr David, he did not tell you?"

"Well, no. He said he would arrange some temporary accommodation for me, until I could sort something out for myself, but I didn't dream he would impose upon anyone to put me up."

"You mind?"

"Of course not. But I wouldn't want to be a nuisance to you."

"No nuisance," said Maggie. "Actually a big help."

"Oh?"

"Of course. One flat. Two tenants. Each pays only half the rent."

"Well, so long as you don't mind."

"I will enjoy the company, and

perhaps improve my English even more."

"I think your English is good enough already."

That obviously pleased Maggie, who went on enthusiastically, "You will like my — *our* — flat, I think. It is quite large by Hong Kong standards, and is located in the North Point district, which makes it very convenient for the journey to work."

Their passage through the Cross-Harbour Tunnel took ten minutes. When they emerged at the other end, they were in Hong Kong itself.

As they left the tunnel behind them, they turned left so that they were following the line of the Hong Kong Mass Transit Railway that wound northeast up to Causeway Bay, Fortress Hill and beyond.

Lauren was amazed that so many buildings of so many different designs could co-exist side-by-side, and that anyone could make order out of so much apparent chaos. People were everywhere. The roads were jammed with all kinds of traffic, from green double-decker buses and trams to Rolls-Royces, rickshaws and bicycles.

Gaudy signs written in both English and Chinese hung across the street to form an arch beneath which they had to travel. Hong Kong was a riot of frenetic activity, all noise and movement, and the smells of sweet, spicy cooking drifted redolently on the muggy air, much of it emanating from the umbrella-covered stalls that lined both pavements.

"My goodness," Lauren said, taken aback by it all, "is it *always* like this?"

Maggie's laugh was musical. "No," she replied. "Sometimes it is even busier."

As the expressway opened out, so the motoring became easier, and soon they left much of the bustle behind them. Some little time later they reached an area in which high-rise apartments rose skyward beside smart villas surrounded by landscaped gardens, and Maggie announced, "We are here."

They parked in the car-park beneath one of the better-tended tenements and struggled Lauren's luggage from the car. Maggie said that their flat was on the ninth floor, overlooking the harbour and the airport from which they had just come, and together they carried the cases to the lift and rode smoothly up to their destination.

Now all the excitement was beginning to work the opposite effect on Lauren, and she began to feel the weariness that all travellers experience once the initial euphoria of arriving in a new country wears off. She had to stifle a yawn as the lift doors slid smoothly open and Maggie led them along a softly-lit, tiled hallway to their front door.

"I will have to get a key cut for you," the Oriental girl remarked as she delved inside her purse.

She unlocked the door and they entered a very clean, though rather spartan apartment. Following Maggie's lead, Lauren set her luggage down in the hallway and allowed herself to be given a brief guided tour.

All the rooms opened off the hall; two bedrooms on one side, the living room, bathroom and kitchen on the other. The decor was simple; plain white walls enlivened here and there by a print or ornament. The furniture was strictly functional. The view from the living room window was something else entirely, though; a sea of junks and sampans plying the bay's waters with their fan-shaped sails set wide, and beyond them the airport, like some gigantic aviary from which metal birds swooped and rose in a constant cycle of movement.

"You like?" Maggie asked quietly.

Lauren turned to face her. "It's marvellous," she replied. "I couldn't be happier to stay here for as long as you'll have me."

"I am pleased. Now, I will see about food. You like Chinese food, Lau-ren?"

"Yes. Is there anything I can do to help, though?"

"No. I will attend to everything. You just relax."

"I think I'll start unpacking," Lauren decided.

It took her a while to carry all of her luggage through to the guest bedroom, which was not really very big. As Maggie had said, however, by Hong Kong standards, where space was at a premium, it was relatively sizeable.

The afternoon was shaping up to be even more sultry, and this too was having a debilitating effect upon her. As she set about unpacking, she realised that she was becoming so weary that she could hardly keep her eyes open, and after a while she decided that unpacking could wait; it might be wiser to stretch out on the bed for a few moments. After all, she didn't want to be suffering the effects of jet-lag when she met David Kent later that afternoon.

The mattress was cool and welcoming. The sounds Maggie made preparing their meal were distant but comforting. A ship's horn sounded somewhere out in the bay. Even up here, on the ninth floor, she could feel the atmosphere of the island. It was somehow different, electric, full of far eastern promise.

Almost before she knew it, sleep had transported her to yet another exotic locale. But this dreamscape held to it nothing of Hong Kong's urbanisation. This was a remote, forested region, where rivers stretched west to east and surplus water emptied out into lakes or marshland. A ricefield spread away to the north. Further east rose mist-cloaked hills — no, not hills, *mountains*, the most enormous, bleak-looking mountains.

She did not know where she was or what she was supposed to be doing here. Somehow, through some hard-to-define insight, though, she knew that the way ahead was marked by a series of hills and valleys.

It came to her then that she was dreaming, but at the same time, how *could* she be dreaming? This place appeared to be so real — why, she could even feel the clammy, warm dampness of the air against her flushed face, see the dark, heavy-bellied clouds gathering in the north.

She heard a sound behind her just then and turned to face a shadowy stand of trees, their thick boles wrapped with lianas and trailing vines. A movement caught her eye and made her tense. A crackling of brush made her start. At last she saw a figure come out of the trees and lift one hand to beckon her. It was a man, tall, sturdily-built, dark-haired and tanned. He called her name.

"Lauren! Lauren! Come here!"

She shook her head, sending a quiver through her blonde hair. "No!"

"But this is madness!"

"Leave me alone!"

"No! I mean it, Lauren! You're

coming back with me!" And so saying, the man began to stride towards her, his long legs eating up the ground that separated them until she could make out more details of his appearance; the midnight blue-black of the hair falling down across his forehead, the light of determination in his deep brown eyes.

"David . . . ?" she mumbled in disbelief.

This was insane! What was David Kent doing out here in the middle of this strange, uncharted wilderness? Where *was* she, anyway? And why was he so insistent about taking her back to . . . wherever?

But there was no time for further questions. Already his big dark shadow was falling across her and he was reaching out to grab hold of her with one strong, long-fingered hand she could not hope to fight off.

"No!" she cried out as she shrank back from him. "*No!*"

The hand came down on her shoulder,

the fingers squeezing insistently. She felt them pressing into her flesh through the material of her dress. She heard his voice calling her name again . . . "Lauren!" . . . but no, not *his* voice, a higher, more feminine voice . . .

"Lau-ren? Lau-ren? Are you all right?"

She opened her eyes with a start, not sure where she was at first. Her heart was hammering unpleasantly. Then she focused on the round, concerned face peering down at her, recognised Maggie and calmed down a little. It *had* been a dream after all, then. But it had been so *vivid* . . .

"Are you all right?" the Chinese girl asked again.

Lauren drew in a deep breath and nodded. "Yes. Must have dozed off, I suppose, had a dream. Or a nightmare."

"I was worried about you," Maggie remarked sincerely. "You sounded as if you were in pain."

Lauren sat up, beginning to feel better though still shaken. "I'm sorry, Maggie. I didn't mean to trouble you. I don't often moan in my sleep, I promise you! But it all seemed so *real* . . . "

"You can tell me about it while we eat, if you like," Maggie invited. "The food is ready."

"There really isn't that much to tell," Lauren replied, getting to her feet. "It was all so strange. Nothing about it made any sense." Gathering her thoughts and putting the dream behind her — or at least trying to — she said, "I'll just wash my face and I'll be right there."

The feel of cold water against her skin completed the transformation, and when she joined Maggie in the kitchen, where they dined on a delicious meal of minced pork dumplings and savoury-filled spring rolls, Lauren was back in control of herself.

Still . . . what did her strange dream mean, if anything? Even now she could remember every detail so clearly. But should she simply dismiss it from her mind — or was Fate trying to tell her about some momentous adventure that still lay in store for her?

2

After they'd finished the washing up, Lauren went to change out of her somewhat travel-creased clothes and into something fresher. She settled on a thin khaki skirt and a white blouse with pockets.

When she was ready, Maggie suggested they make their way to the *Ex-Pat*'s office. "I know Mr David will be pleased to see that you have arrived safely."

Lauren's smile faltered. Mention of the *Ex-Pat* editor's name had brought the strange dream back to her. But Lauren was nothing if not practical and level-headed. As unsettling as the dream had been, her sleep had refreshed her, and the food had further revitalised her. Dreams were just dreams after all. They had no precognitive significance at all.

"Just let me get my bag, then, and we'll go," she replied brightly.

On the way down in the lift, Maggie said, "We have moved offices quite recently, although we are still in the Central District. Traffic is very heavy there, so it is best if we take the tram."

The afternoon was muggy. It appeared that Lauren had arrived in the middle of a heatwave. Fortunately, however, the tram wasn't too crowded, and a whisper of a breeze filtered in through the open doors and windows once they got underway.

"This is a big step you have taken," Maggie remarked after a while. "Travelling all this way for a job. You are to be admired."

Lauren had been watching the scenery flash by. Now she glanced at her companion. "It was an opportunity that was too good to miss. Back home I was just plodding along, going through the motions. Here, I hope I'll be able to do some *real* reporting at last."

"But what of your family? They do not mind that you have come so far to work?"

"Of course not. They want what I want."

"And your boyfriend also?"

"I don't have a boyfriend."

The admission suddenly made Lauren realise that she had *never* had a boyfriend. Oh, she'd had friends who were boys — men — but it wasn't really the same thing. There had not been the same easy togetherness in those relationships, that special intimacy.

Not that Lauren felt that she had missed out on anything. She had never really given much thought to anything except her career. Now, though . . . Maybe it was just the fact that she was a stranger in a strange land that was increasing her sense of isolation and making her wish . . . what? That she had someone with whom to share this new phase in her life? Yes.

"That is good, perhaps," Maggie

said, breaking in on her thoughts. "A boyfriend might not have wanted you to leave your country."

"That's right," Lauren agreed without much conviction. "What about you, Maggie? Do *you* have a boyfriend?"

Maggie's broad grin was as infectious as ever. "He lives in the New Territories, near my parents," she explained, blushing like a teenager. "Tsim Sha Tsui. You have heard of it, yes? His name is Jackie Lo. We are . . . how do you say it? Pledged?"

Lauren decided to play the Chinese girl at her own game. "Pledged," she said. "Engaged. Affianced. Betrothed. Promised."

Maggie laughed.

After a while the traffic began to build up as Maggie had said it would, and Lauren craned her neck for a better look at the Central District, which was the real hub of Hong Kong.

Skyscrapers rose up everywhere. Many of them seemed to be banks, or banking headquarters. Lauren also spotted government buildings, and though most of the structures appeared to be quite modern, she also saw an old, colonial-style courthouse.

That familiar excitement began to make her tingle again. What a marvellous city in which to work! She knew for sure now that she had made the right decision to come here, knew that she had been right to give up her boring life in London to enjoy this great centre of commerce. Already she had never felt more alive.

When they reached their stop, they climbed down from the tram and Maggie led them along bustling Connaught Road Central, where fountains spewed white water into the air on their right. Lauren wanted to take in every sight and sound at once, but cautioned herself to go slowly. There would be time enough to see the city over the next six months. Besides, if she was to be working right here in the heart of the island itself . . .

Maggie took them across a busy

road, somehow managing to avoid all the traffic, and they continued on along another grand thoroughfare.

Expectation rose still higher in Lauren. Now that all of this was becoming a reality, she began to wonder about her working environment. It was too much to expect that she would have her own office, but what of her desk? Would it be large or small? She could picture it in her mind, possibly the biggest desk in the world, with one of the top-range word processors perched on one corner; an in-tray; an out-tray; a spotless blotter; a positive switchboard of coloured telephones, each one the key to a contact with the most amazing scoop for her.

And what of these cloud-touching buildings? Which of these belonged to her newspaper? *Her* newspaper!

Maggie turned into a sidestreet and Lauren followed dutifully. But this street was a world away from those they had just left behind them. The tall buildings surrounding them dwarfed these frankly rather uninspiring, antiquated brown-brick structures, and left them in a constant grey shadow all day long.

Still, Lauren was not unduly concerned. This was doubtless just a short-cut, what was known locally as a 'go-down'. But then Maggie slowed down when they came to possibly the most dilapidated building in the block and gestured with one hand. "We are here," she said.

Lauren peered up at the pile, horrified. "This?" she replied when she was able to find her voice. "This . . . is . . . it?"

Clearly Maggie could not understand her reaction. "Yes," she replied almost proudly.

"But . . . " The English girl had to search for the right phrase, but when at last she found it, she realised that to voice it would be to make the cub reporter's error; to judge a book by its cover. And who knew what wonders this old building might be hiding behind its drab exterior? She must wait and see exactly what lay beyond these paint-peeling double-doors before saying something she might soon regret.

"Shall we, ah . . . go inside?" she suggested with little real enthusiasm.

Maggie led the way, up five worn stone steps and into a rather dingy-looking reception area where an emaciated Oriental man in his late sixties was reading a racing sheet.

He looked up at the newcomers through rheumy eyes, his somewhat guarded appraisal of Lauren quickly replaced by a smile for Maggie. Nodding his head in her direction, he greeted the Chinese girl with an enquiry. "*Nin hao. Nei ho ma?*"

"*Gay ho, nei yau sum,*" Maggie replied.

An elevator stood to one side of a dark set of stairs. The two girls stepped into the elevator and Maggie pulled the doors closed behind them and pressed the button for the second floor. The lift wheezed and rattled into movement, slowly clawing its way up the shaft.

Somewhere at the top of the building came the screaming and yelling of children at play. It echoed weirdly down the grimy shaft, and gave Lauren quite a jolt. "What — !"

"We share building with many other tenants," Maggie explained with a smile. "The one you can hear now is a day nursery."

"And that odd rattling sound?"

"Sewing machines. There is a clothing manufacturer on the first floor."

Lauren was finding it difficult to feel optimistic now. Whatever hope she'd had that this dilapidated old building hid a totally modern workplace was evaporating fast. She remembered that Maggie had told her that the *Ex-Pat* had moved offices recently. She wondered why, and what the old offices must have been like, and was just about to ask when the elevator ground to a shuddering halt at the second floor and Maggie pushed the doors aside.

They stepped out into a single

large room which was jammed with heavy old dark-wood desks, most of them unoccupied but nonetheless overflowing with paperwork.

Lauren came to a halt almost at once, her clear blue eyes filled now with disbelief as she glanced around the room. Whatever she had been expecting, this was most certainly not it.

Two fans turned sluggishly in the high ceiling. The dull green walls were covered in a chaotic variety of clippings, calendars, memos, photographs clipped from magazines and the ubiquitous, but in this case probably sadly accurate sampler which read; YOU DON'T HAVE TO BE MAD TO WORK HERE, BUT IT HELPS.

Four people occupied the room, all Caucasian men in their late thirties or early forties. One of them was talking into a telephone, using some cumbersome form of pidgin-Cantonese to make himself understood. Another was pecking away at a vintage typewriter, apparently making a mistake with every other word. A tall, long-haired fellow was standing at a drawing board in the corner, pasting up the front page of the next edition of the *Ex-Pat*. The fourth man appeared to be dozing in the languid heat.

"Come," said Maggie.

They weaved around all the paper-choked desks and headed for an open door in the opposite wall. The men watched their passage, but not one of them offered a greeting. Behind them, an old Bakelite telephone began to ring, but no-one made any attempt to answer it.

Maggie paused in the doorway and tapped gently against one of the portal's clear glass panels. Almost at once a strong, quite pleasant voice said, "Come."

They went into a small but equally chaotic office that was dominated by a large old desk awash with paperwork and several filing cabinets, all of them crammed so tight that the drawers refused to close flush.

Seated at the desk, head bent, engrossed in checking copy, sat David Kent.

As Lauren followed Maggie inside, the first thing she saw was that mop of raven-black hair, remembered so well from her interview and seen again so recently in her strange dream. At last he reached the bottom of the typewritten page and looked up, and the breath caught slightly in her throat as she came face to face with him again after so long.

Recognition dawned in his dark brown eyes and at once a smile tugged at lips used to good humour. He stood up, revealing his generous height, and came hurriedly around the desk with his right hand extended in greeting. His white shirt was a startling contrast to the bronze of his clear skin. Its sleeves were rolled back to reveal his firm, golden forearms, his maroon tie pulled loose at the throat to reveal a few dark hairs growing high across his upper chest.

"Lauren!" he said with what appeared to be genuine warmth. "It's good to see you again! Please, come in, have a seat." He realised that the visitor's chair was stacked with old editions of the *Ex-Pat* and hurriedly moved to scoop them up and deposit them in an unsightly heap on the floor. "Did you have a good flight?" he asked as she sat down.

"Fine, thank you, Mr Kent," she said rather formally.

"David, please. And no problems with your visa or work permit?"

"No."

"Good, good," he said as he retook his seat on the other side of the desk, his beaming smile making him appear much younger than his thirty-two years. "Well, I imagine you must still be pretty tired after your flight. When did you get in?"

"About two hours ago."

"All right; I'll give you the edited highlights of my standard 'welcome aboard' speech, then," he decided around a most appealing grin. "Not that there's much to tell. We're a fairly small operation, as you probably saw on your way in, and we have a circulation figure to match. But we do have our moments. Right now we're in the middle of designing a completely new look for the paper."

He reached into his pocket for a handkerchief with which to mop his face. Somewhere behind him the outdated plumbing gave an ugly rattle and clank. "Can you fetch us a couple of cold drinks, please, Maggie?"

With a little nod, Maggie left the room.

"I won't bore you with all the facts and figures," he went on. "At the moment I imagine you could use a few hours' uninterrupted sleep more. So today I'll show you around and introduce you to the rest of the fellows, and then I suggest you take the rest of the week to acclimatise yourself before starting afresh here on Monday morning." His grin widened. "No need to look so worried. We'll ease you in gently enough, I promise. You can start with some debt-chasing. You know the kind of thing; phoning advertisers to see why they haven't paid their bills yet. Routine stuff, of course, but necessary, I'm afraid."

She frowned. "Excuse me, Mr Kent."

"Yes, Lauren?"

"I think we're at cross purposes. I was employed as a features writer — not a debt collector."

His smile only grew infuriatingly wider. "I know that, Lauren," he replied mildly. "And please — it's David. But you'll have to get to know the city before you can write about it. That'll take you a week or two, at the very least. And like it or not, debt-chasing's a chore that *has* to be done."

"I appreciate that," Lauren replied firmly. "But by a junior member of staff, Mr Kent. *Not* the features writer."

He studied her closely, a bit surprised

by the iron in her tone. "I don't know what you've been used to in London," he responded after a while. "But we do things a bit differently out here. As I said, we're a small outfit. We all have to be adaptable. Besides which, I like my staff to get to know every aspect of the newspaper they're working on."

"But — "

He raised one hand. "The facts are these, Lauren. We take a lot of advertising. We *have* to, in order to show a decent profit at the end of every quarter. But all the advertising in the world's no good to us unless the advertisers settle their accounts on time. That's why it's important for someone to chase them regularly."

"Me," she said softly.

"As the junior member of staff, yes."

"Junior!" For Lauren, that was the last straw. "Mr Kent," she said irritably. "May I be frank?"

"Of course."

"I'm a bit surprised by all this."

"Surprised?"

"Surprised," said a familiar voice over by the door. "Amazed. Speechless. Thunderstruck. Caught on the hop."

Lauren and David both turned to face Maggie, who had just returned with two soft drinks. The smile on the Chinese girl's face faded a little as she sensed the atmosphere in the small office, and she quickly set down the drinks and beat a hasty retreat.

"Surprised, Lauren?" David Kent asked again, curiously.

"At this place," she replied, taking a deep breath. "My job. It's not quite what I expected. What I was led to expect at my interview."

"Oh?"

"To be honest with you, Mr Kent, I'm beginning to feel as if I've been dragged all this way under false pretences."

He looked at her for a long, silent moment, his tanned face very serious. At last he said, "Do you, now? And why is that?"

She could not suppress a snort of

disbelief. "Why? Isn't that perfectly obvious, Mr Kent?"

"David," he reminded her.

Ignoring him, she went on. "I came here to work on a newspaper. By your own admission, I now discover that *The Ex-Pat* is really just a vehicle for advertisers, little more than another glorified free-sheet. I expected to work in a half-way civilised environment. Instead I find the paper being produced from possibly the most run-down, seedy, worn-out building in all of Hong Kong. And although I was employed as a features writer, I now understand that I am expected to work as a debt-collector as well."

"*Chaser*," he corrected. "There's a difference."

But she was not about to be distracted. "To be perfectly honest with you, Mr Kent, I'm beginning to think I might have been better off where I was."

When he was sure that she had finished her tirade, he said, "I hope you feel better now that you've got all that off your chest."

"I'd sooner you didn't patronise me, Mr Kent."

"David," he said easily. "And I have no intention of patronising you. But I *will* overlook that little outburst of yours, because you've just arrived and the journey's probably taken more out of you than you know and you're just not thinking straight."

"There's nothing wrong with my thinking," she said haughtily.

"All right," he replied with a shrug. "There's nothing wrong with your thinking. We'll write it off as inexperience, then."

"Inexperience?" she said incredulously.

"Naiveté," he explained.

She was outraged now. Nothing hurt worse than not being taken seriously. "You will most certainly not write it off, Mr Kent — "

"David."

" — to inexperience or anything else!"

"All right," he said again, as easy-going as ever. "We'll get a few things straight right now, so there'll be no more misunderstandings between us." He got to his feet and reached for one of the soft drinks. "In the first place, you came to work on a newspaper, and that's exactly what *The Ex-Pat* is — a damned fine newspaper. Of course, we run adverts. What journal doesn't? It's a good source of revenue and our readers seem to like them.

"You came here expecting to work in glamorous surroundings. Well, I'm sorry that we don't quite come up to scratch, but it's all a question of economics, Lauren."

"Miss Adams," she corrected primly.

"Rents here in Hong Kong are among the highest in the world," he continued, unabashed. "If I have to choose between losing two members of staff or moving to cheaper offices, I move to cheaper offices. It's my experience that we can operate just as well here as in some fancy high-rise.

47

"And as for your being employed as a features writer — all right; write me a feature on some aspect of Hong Kong." He drank from his paper cup. "Well? Any ideas yet?"

She sat there, beginning to feel wretched.

"Lauren?" he prompted.

"Miss Adams," she replied defiantly.

"What will you write about?" he asked harshly.

She mumbled her reply.

"What was that?"

"I don't know," she repeated, louder.

"And you *won't* know, either," he said, moderating his tone. "Until you get to know the city. Which will take time." He sat down again. "Do you understand the position now — *Miss* Adams?"

Her blue eyes flashed dangerously. "Do you *like* humiliating people?" she asked in a low voice.

"It's not a question of humiliating you," he replied. "But I think it's as well that you learn a few home truths before we go any further." He softened his tone in an attempt to take the sting out of his words. "Look, I don't want an argument any more than I think *you* do. It's too hot, for one thing. But think back to your interview. Did I even *once* tell you that *The Ex-Pat* was something it wasn't? Did I tell you that we operated from the plushest building in Hong Kong? Lauren . . . you do me a serious injustice if you believe I'm the kind of man who would deliberately drag someone halfway around the world on the strength of a pack of lies."

She, too, lost some of her fire when she realised the truth of his words; realised also that she had allowed her imagination to run away with her and heighten her expectations. "I didn't mean to imply that," she said softly. "I'm sorry, Mr Kent. Perhaps I'd better go, before I make an even bigger fool of myself."

"Hold on, now. There's no need for that."

"I think there is," she replied, getting to her feet.

"Where are you going, then?" he demanded, anger and impatience creeping back into his tone.

She shrugged, picking up her shoulder-bag. She had made such an idiot of herself that she could not bring herself to look him in the face. "I really *am* sorry to have wasted your time, Mr Kent. Goodbye."

"Lauren!"

She stopped at the door and looked back at him over her shoulder. She had no desire to have him rub salt in her wounds. She already felt bad enough. She had just ruined that chance of a lifetime she had spent two months of her life being so proud of. He was right; she *was* naive. But knowing that did not make the awful, sorry truth of it any easier to bear.

He opened his mouth to say something more, but she was so upset that she wanted only to leave this wretched building behind her and lose herself among Hong Kong's teeming millions.

She turned away from him and left the office, hurrying around all the accumulated desks outside and ignoring the curious looks of the other *Ex-Pat* employees but feeling their eyes on her nonetheless, until she reached the frail old elevator and made her desperate escape from this once-sweet dream that had all-too-rapidly turned sour.

3

It took Lauren a minute, possibly less, to lose herself in the crowd. The Central District, with its maze upon maze of busy streets and intersections soon swallowed her whole.

Quickly she put as much distance as she could between herself and the *Ex-Pat* offices, until eventually her raging emotions began to calm down.

Here in these bustling streets she found the anonymity she craved so desperately. The way she had behaved in front of David Kent was a painful memory now, but a memory nonetheless. She could not go back in time and do everything differently. She must accept the facts as they were and make the best of them. Why, she might even be able to turn this change in her fortunes to her advantage, though she knew that this would be impossible, that she was only trying to make herself feel better.

She was in the rather European-sounding Des Voeux Road now, and her attention was taken by an impressive five-storey complex called The Landmark, which appeared to house an endless procession of shops. Seeking refuge in distraction, she turned into the shopping centre and allowed the sights and sounds of the city to console her still further. After a while she went into a brightly-lit coffee shop and sat by the window, where she nursed a cup of delicate Chinese tea and tried to gather her thoughts.

But sitting still only gave her more time to think. How foolishly she had behaved! It would be nice to believe that David Kent had been right about the flight having tired her out, to dismiss her outburst as something of little consequence that was soon — and best — forgotten. But Lauren knew better. Like a child she had allowed her thoughts to be coloured by an over-active imagination, and just like a *spoilt* child she had acted abominably when reality had failed to match fantasy.

Still, there was little to be gained from continuing to replay the events of the afternoon through her mind. She had ruined her big chance. That was all that mattered, the one basic fact she must learn to live with.

But now a new thought occurred to her. What would her family and friends — well, acquaintances really, since she had always been rather too single-minded in her objectives to make friends — think of her when she came home so soon, Lauren the great journalist?

Despair threatened to overwhelm her again, and before it could do exactly that she stood up and hurried across to the cash register, intending to pay her tab.

"Oh!"

It was in that moment that she realised she had not yet changed any of her British currency for Hong Kong dollars.

Her shoulders slumped. Very suddenly she felt close to tears, because that was the final indignity, having to go up to the prim-faced Chinese woman at the cash desk and explain just how stupid she had really been.

But there was nothing to be gained by delaying the admission, so, with a sigh, she continued on towards the counter, where she cleared her throat and said in Chinese, "Excuse me. I seem to have run into a spot of bother . . . "

The Chinese woman eyed her guardedly from her perch behind the cash desk, her expression as inscrutable as that of Buddha himself. "Bother?" she asked carefully.

Lauren forced a smile that was intended to put the old woman at ease and assure her that the problem was only minor. "I've just realised," she said, continuing to use the Chinese she had been practising more and more over the last two months, "I only arrived here this afternoon. I haven't had a chance to change my money up yet."

The Chinese woman understood that, all right. "You must pay bill," she insisted sharply, making some of the coffee shop's other customers look up curiously, only adding to Lauren's embarrassment. Lauren shook her head. "Yes, I know that," she said, keeping her voice low. "I *want* to pay. But all I have is this." She produced a five-pound note to illustrate her problem, just in case her command of Chinese was not as good as she believed it to be. "Can I pay you in English currency?"

A waiter with very dark hair and a frankly suspicious look on his long, thin face appeared at Lauren's shoulder. "There is a problem here?" he asked in halting English.

She turned to face him, wondering how something so simple could become so complicated, but before she could answer him he said, "You have a complaint?"

She shook her head. "No, I — "

"She does not want to pay her

bill," the woman at the cash desk said venomously.

"I never said that!" Lauren gasped indignantly.

The waiter eyed her sternly, his disapproval obvious. "You must pay your bill," he cautioned firmly, "otherwise I will have to call the management."

"That won't be necessary," said a new voice.

All eyes turned to the newcomer, who had just entered the shop. They saw a tall man in his early thirties, tanned, athletic, with his shirtsleeves rolled back and his maroon tie loosened at the throat.

Lauren's eyes went wide. "Mr Kent!"

His smile was little more than a twitch of the lips. "David," he corrected her in that easy, pleasant way of his. "You're not leaving already, are you, Miss Adams? You've only just arrived."

"But — "

Turning his attention to the waiter, the handsome newspaper editor said,

"*Yee laai tcha, m goi.*"

The waiter nodded, all trace of his former hostility gone now, and hurried away to fetch them fresh tea, and when Lauren made no immediate move to return to the table she had just vacated, David reached out to rest a guiding hand on her elbow. "Come on," he said pleasantly.

With little choice in the matter, Lauren made her way back to her table, at once both glad that David had turned up before that business with the currency got entirely out of hand, but embarrassed, too, that she should have to face him again.

"How . . . how did you know where to find me?" she asked as they took seats opposite each other. Her heart was racing madly and her thoughts were still in a whirl, partly due to the events of the last few minutes and partly because his gentle touch had affected her in a most unsettling, but not unpleasant, way.

"You didn't think I'd just let you

58

run off like that, did you?"

"You followed me," she guessed.

"As best I could," he replied with a chuckle. "Though you're pretty fast on your feet, Miss Adams. I lost you twice. Then, as luck would have it, I caught sight of you just as you came into The Landmark. After that it was just a question of finding out which of the stores you'd gone into."

She didn't know whether to feel grateful to him for his consideration, or to resent his following her because it was an invasion of privacy. There was no denying that he had rescued her from a potentially embarrassing scene, though, so she confessed, "It's lucky for me that you found me when you did."

The waiter brought their fresh tea, then left them alone.

"I really *am* sorry, Mr Kent. About earlier, I mean."

"I told you; don't give it another thought," he replied.

"But you don't understand — "

"Of course I do," he insisted. "I've been there myself, don't forget. You're young. You're ambitious. You're anxious to make your mark, and you feel that everything has to be done against the clock." He shook his head. "If only you knew. You've all the time in the world."

She eyed him curiously. "That sounds as if you speak with the voice of experience, Mr Kent."

"David."

Her smile chased some of the unhappiness from her face. "All right — David."

"Experience?" He considered the word for a moment as he tried his tea. "Oh, I've had the experience, all right. Went to work for my local paper straight from school. Started off as a general dogsbody. Moved around a bit, found out what it was like in telesales, advertising, production, the morgue, and finally features."

"Then how did you end up here?"

"On just about the dullest, coldest,

most rain-soaked Monday morning for a hundred years, the paper I worked on made about half the workforce redundant, me included. I was about your age then, and I took it as a personal insult. After all, hadn't I given them seven years of my life? I was ambitious myself in those days. I wanted to climb and keep on climbing, and I resented the fact that my bosses didn't think I was worth keeping on."

Something painful crossed his face then, which he quickly masked. "It can have a very sobering effect on you, losing your job. I became very morose. But when I finally got everything into perspective, I realised that all that ambition, all the personal sacrifices I'd made to climb the ladder, hadn't got me anywhere. After a couple of weeks, though, I realised I was a happier person *without* all that ambition nagging away at me. So maybe my old bosses did me a favour the day they gave me my marching orders."

She was fascinated by this insight into him. "I still don't understand," she pressed. "How did you end up here?"

"Simple. I decided to use my redundancy money to see something of the world before settling down to look for another job. I got as far as Hong Kong and then I fell in love."

Lauren, in the act of reaching for her cup, paused then. She knew a strange and unaccountable sensation of disappointment, because up to now she had automatically assumed that he was free and unattached. The sudden discovery that he was either married, engaged or already involved in a relationship jarred her curiously, and she found the knowledge strangely hurtful.

Before she could question her emotions, she heard herself saying, "You fell in love?"

He nodded. "With the city."

Her sudden surge of relief was as irrational as just about every other emotion David Kent had brought out in her so far, but that didn't make it any less welcome. But at once fresh questions came into her confused mind. That he was an attractive man was inescapable. But that in itself was a remarkable and unusual observation for her to make, because she had never before really considered much beyond her desire to succeed in her chosen career.

Perhaps she, too, was learning that ambition was not everything.

"So you stayed here," she said, reaching for her cup. "And went to work for *The Ex-Pat*."

"That's right," he agreed. "More or less. But that's enough about me. It's *you* we have to sort out."

Her mood, which had lightened a little, now darkened again. "I didn't mean to sound so high-and-mighty back at your office," she told him sincerely. "I suppose I was expecting too much. To have come all this way . . . I felt, well — let down."

"You'll achieve everything you want,

in time," he predicted. "But there's no substitute for experience and patience. You have to learn to walk before you can learn to run, remember. And though we might look a little rough around the edges, we're one of the best newspapers of our type you're likely to find anywhere."

"I realise that now," she said ruefully.

"I've seen your work," he went on. "I know you can write. What I want you to do for me now is come back to the office and let me introduce you to the others."

She thought about that, struggling to contain a growing panic.

"I know you feel embarrassed," he said softly, and with a gentle understanding she found both comforting and attractive. "It *was* a pretty dramatic exit you made, after all. But if you *really* want to make it as a newspaperwoman . . . "

Her full lips curved into a smile. "I do."

"Then how about it? Before they all

push off early behind my back?"

Reaching her decision, she nodded firmly. "All right . . . David. I really *do* want to make a go of this. But I'll only go on one condition."

He eyed her in mild surprise. "Yes, Miss Adams?"

Her smile broadened. "That you start to call me Lauren."

His smile matched hers, and as she looked into his eyes she knew a contentment that was as new to her as this sprawling city.

"Lauren," he said, standing up. "You just made yourself a deal."

★ ★ ★

The next few days were a kaleidoscope of new sights and sounds as Lauren made the most of her free time before starting her new job. David Kent had told her she would have to get to know the city before she could write about it, and that was exactly what she intended to do.

Each morning she left the flat and took a tram to any one of Hong Kong's four districts, and there she would observe, make copious notes, engage some of the locals in conversation as a means of improving her own fluency in Chinese, and strike up conversations with tourists in order to get their perspective, too. She walked the streets and parks of the island, sampled the buses, trains and underground railway, and gradually began to develop a feel for the colony. As single-minded as ever, she gave herself completely to this new phase of her career.

Each night she returned to the flat feeling exhausted but satisfied with a job well done. By the time she reported for work first thing on Monday morning, she had improved her understanding of the city no end.

On her way into work on that first day she felt just a little bit nervous, but not so bad now that David had introduced her to her colleagues. First appearances had certainly been deceptive, she now realised. As David had explained on their way back from the coffee shop on that first tumultuous day in Hong Kong, "They're bachelors, all of them. And as you probably noticed earlier on, they're not exactly house-proud."

"Not *exactly*," she replied dryly.

"I think that, being a woman, they're afraid you'll want to make changes, bring a sense of orderliness to the place — and if there's one thing we bachelors dread, it's change."

She glanced up at his profile as they continued on along the crowded, sun-splashed street, puzzled and a little bit disturbed by the strange excitement the discovery of his single status had aroused in her. Ever the realist, she told herself that she was allowing her imagination to run wild again, that being in this exotic new land with this handsome and charming man was threatening to fill her head with romance. After all, she had never given it much thought before this. But then again, she had never met a man like David Kent before this.

But there she went again! This was ridiculous. How *could* she be attracted to this man? She hardly knew anything about him! She must get it out of her system once and for all and concentrate on more important matters; her career, for example.

Still . . . there *was* something about him, the ivory flash of his easy grin, the promise of humour in his depthless brown eyes, his intelligence and compassion and masculinity, that stirred a hitherto-dormant desire in Lauren, a desire to feel the soft brush of his lips, the comforting power of his embrace —

With a determined effort she banished all thought of romance and relationships from her mind. From now on she must keep her mind firmly on her work — and make sure that the only relationship they enjoyed was a purely business one.

That first week fairly flew by. Lauren

made it her business to learn the routines of the office and to fit in as well as she could. And as soon as they realised that she was not about to disrupt the organised chaos of their work-place, she found it easy to create a pleasant rapport with her colleagues. Indeed, they could not have been any friendlier to her had they tried, and she was secretly pleased to have been accepted by them so well.

She also got debt-chasing down to a fine art, and was soon able to make a noticeable reduction in the number of advertisers who had not settled their accounts.

Still, David had been right; everyone in the office was quite capable of filling in for the rest. Adaptability really *was* the key-word, for *The Ex-Pat* was a smaller operation than she had realised. Having said that, however, she was profoundly impressed by the paper they were able to put out each week for Hong Kong's more than 20,000 British residents. Given time, she really felt that she could go places here.

At the end of the week Lauren submitted a small, humorous article on the perils of forgetting to change up one's currency, and much to her delight, David promised to publish it in the following week's edition.

Deciding to push her luck, she said, "Uh . . . David . . . that's something I've been meaning to talk to you about."

It was late on Friday afternoon and they were in his office. The weather was still hot and dry, but by now she was growing accustomed to the constant humidity.

The usual seemingly-disorganised rush to put the latest edition of the paper to bed was behind them for one more week, and he was feeling quite expansive and open to offers.

"Yes, Lauren?"

"I've been working on a feature I'd like you to take a look at."

He eyed her with interest, because he hadn't discussed any potential subjects with her yet, and had been content to let her familiarise herself with her new environment for a couple of weeks. "Oh?"

She nodded. "Yes. I . . . well, you told me to get to know the city before I tried writing about it."

"And now you have," he said.

"Yes." She put a manilla envelope on the desk in front of him and said, "Perhaps you'll take a look at it when you get a spare moment."

"Sure."

"Well . . . " She felt uncharacteristically shy in front of him, because try as she might, she had been unable to stifle her attraction towards him. He really *was* a hard person not to like. But unfortunately for Lauren, it was not just a case of 'like'. It was something much stronger. "I'll, ah, see you on Monday, then," she finished lamely.

He nodded, and when he smiled her pulse began to race.

She was almost to the door when he called her name. She turned at once, her expression curious and perhaps a little eager. "Yes?"

"Have a nice weekend."

She paused before replying, not sure if there had been something else behind his words or expression, a kind of wistfulness that he would not be sharing the break with her — a wistfulness she shared. But then she decided that her imagination was playing tricks on her again, and at last she said, "And you."

It was only when Lauren got back to the flat that she remembered that Maggie had said she was going home for the weekend, as she usually did. It looked as if she, Lauren, had a lonely couple of days ahead of her, then, and sure enough, when she let herself into the apartment, she was struck by the emptiness and utter silence of the place.

The flat was stuffy, so she opened a few windows. Traffic-sounds floated up to her from down below, the purr and growl of car engines, the occasional impatient blare of a horn. For a time she just stood there by the windows, her mood reflective, her vista — that of the busy Victoria Harbour — still magnificent enough to take her breath away.

She wondered what to do with herself this coming weekend. She had already explored much of Hong Kong and the New Territories. Perhaps she would do some shopping and write a few letters and postcards home.

She decided to take a shower to help her unwind from the pressures of the day, and afterwards, clad only in a peach-coloured silk dressing-gown, she made herself a cup of tea and went to lounge on the sofa, deciding that she would eat later, when it cooled down a little and she had more of an appetite.

It had been a hard week, and now, at the end of it, the demands of it began to take their toll. As the amber sun began its regal slide beyond the western horizon and the neat little living-room slowly darkened, so Lauren felt her eyelids take on extra weight.

Almost before she realised it, she had fallen asleep. She knew that she was dreaming as soon as she found herself on the strange, endless plain she had encountered in the dream she'd had on her first day in Hong Kong, but she knew the fact only in some vague and not especially immediate way. And in any case, she was too curious and, yes, just a little alarmed, to comfort herself with the knowledge.

Slowly she turned in a circle. Yes, everything was exactly the same as it had been in that first, puzzling dream. Here was that marshy expanse stretching away in one grass-spiked puddle after another. There, to the north, was the rice-field, and there to the east rose the misty blue mountains, bleak, sombre and unclimbable.

Again she was struck by the absolute reality of her surroundings. She could feel the damp warmth of the air on her face, hear the distant, raucous cries of ascending birds as they lifted heavenward to the south. Everything was so vivid, *too* vivid to be dismissed as just a dream.

But what did it mean? What was her subconscious trying to tell her?

She came to a halt before the dense forest of vine and liana-wrapped trees, trying to think the whole thing through, see some sense in the mystery of it. That was when she heard the crackling sounds of someone coming out of the green darkness of the forest.

She jumped, even though she knew the identity of the newcomer. Instinctively she took a few paces away from the shivering undergrowth until suddenly she could make out a dark shape shifting among the shadows, an ill-defined silhouette that jumped without warning into sharper focus, the figure of a man, tall, athletic, with dark hair and a winning smile —

A smile pulled at her own lips, a smile filled with anticipation and longing. Her mouth opened to whisper his name, "*David* . . . "

But — no! She gasped. It *wasn't* David! She had never seen this man before, although he had about him a strange familiarity. And though his smile was broad and seemingly sincere, and his brown, Oriental's eyes held only the promise of care and attention, she somehow felt that he was not to be trusted . . . in fact, just the opposite . . . that he was to be *feared* . . .

4

"Uh? Wh-what — ?"

Lauren did not know if it was the sudden realisation that the strange man in her dream was not to be trusted that woke her up, or the insistent buzzing of the doorbell. When at last her eyelids snapped open, however, she knew one thing for certain; that she had evidently been asleep for some time, because the living-room was now appreciably darker than it had been when she had first closed her eyes.

She sat up, still confused and unsettled by her dream, although some of the finer details were already growing faint and difficult to recollect.

The doorbell buzzed again.

Lauren glanced up at the clock over the mantel. It was 8:45.

She frowned. Still vaguely disoriented by the dream, she felt a stab of alarm.

Who would be calling at this time of night? But then she allowed herself to relax. It was probably one of Maggie's friends, unaware that she had gone away for the weekend. Even so, Lauren went out into the hallway on tip-toe, and once at the door, called out cautiously, "Yes? Who's there?"

A voice called back, "Lauren?"

She frowned.

"Lauren, is that you? It's me — David Kent."

Now she really *was* puzzled. What was David doing here? She wondered if everything were all right at the office. Hurriedly she unbolted the door and opened it. Almost immediately he brushed past her and went straight through to the living-room, his face tight with what appeared to be anger.

"David?" she asked, concerned. She closed the door behind him and quickly hurried into the living-room, where he was waiting impatiently. "David?" she said again. "What is it? Is something wrong?"

She had only ever seen him in shirts and ties before. Now he was dressed casually in a pale blue polo shirt and a pair of light-grey cotton trousers. There was nothing casual about his expression, however. His brown eyes fairly burned into her, and in his right hand he was clutching an envelope so tightly that the paper was bending beneath the pressure of his fingers.

"Yes," he said at last, his voice low and sharp. "Yes, Lauren, there *is* something wrong. This." And so saying, he threw the envelope down on the coffee table.

She shook her head. "I don't understand — "

"The article you gave me just before you went home," he said. "The piece you did on illegal dentists."

Her voice grew guarded. "What about it?"

"What about it?" He snorted. "Do I really need to tell you?"

"I think perhaps you'd better," she said, adding meaningfully, "*After*

79

you've apologised for your behaviour so far."

That seemed to jar some of the antagonism from him, and it was almost as if he was only now beginning to realise exactly where he was.

He nodded. "Yes, you're right," he said quietly. "I was forgetting myself. I'm sorry. I hope I haven't disturbed you. I appreciate that I'm encroaching on your free time, and I won't take up any more of it than I have to. But I think we'd better get a few things straight."

"About my article?"

His nod was short, brisk and all business. "Yes."

She frowned. What could she possibly have written that had brought out such a reaction in him? Unable to obtain licenses from the Hong Kong government, or to qualify at their profession in China, many dentists had set up their illegal surgeries near the so-called Walled City in Kowloon, where they performed suspect and often dangerous operations. As soon as Lauren had heard about the trade on her travels the previous week, she had decided to investigate further. The article — two thousand words explaining how the present situation had evolved — had been designed as a warning to residents and tourists alike to avoid the place.

"I'm sorry, David, but I can't see the problem. Didn't you like the piece?"

"Of course I liked it," he replied snappishly. "It was one of the most thoroughly-researched and well-written features it's ever been my pleasure to read."

"Then you'll use it?"

"Certainly."

"Then . . . I'm sorry, but I don't understand. What's the problem?"

"The problem, Lauren, is simply this — to research this piece so well, you must have gone to the Walled City and interviewed some of these charlatans personally. Am I right?"

She paused a moment before

admitting, "Yes."

"And inevitably your research took you *inside* the Walled City?"

"Of course."

He shook his head, clearly exasperated. "Didn't you understand the risk you were taking? The Walled City is taboo to most people. Even the authorities think twice before they go into the place! It's a disorganised maze of seedy backstreets lacking even the most basic of amenities. It's home to all manner of criminals. Even the greenest, most inexperienced tourist knows better than to visit that place!"

"But I was perfectly safe . . . "

"Safe!"

She refused to concede the point. "Well, I didn't come to any harm," she pointed out.

"No," he agreed. "Thank God. But I don't think you realise just how lucky you were!" He paused, trying to curb his rising temper and sound more reasonable. "Look, see it from my point of view. As your editor, I'm responsible for your safety. I know I can't wrap you in cotton wool. I wouldn't want to. But I have to stop you from taking unnecessary risks."

"And going to the Walled City was an unnecessary risk?"

"If you knew as much as you *think* you know," he said, "you wouldn't need to ask that."

"Perhaps I enjoy a little danger," she said defiantly.

It went very quiet in the living-room then, and Lauren realised just how dark it had become with the approach of dusk. A sense of electricity entered the air as he stood looking at her, and she realised that she was standing there before him clad only in a silk dressing-gown that moulded itself to her every curve in such a way that little was left to the imagination.

To her surprise, however, that knowledge only emboldened her, and in some distant, detached part of her mind, she marvelled at her lack of embarrassment. At that moment, every other consideration save the basic facts that he was a man and she was a woman, was washed away. This little flat high above Hong Kong's busy streets was a world in itself, a universe all of their own, and they might have been the only two people on the planet in that snapshot of time.

"You like to live dangerously, do you?" he said softly.

She did not reply. Her mouth had gone so dry, her throat so tight, that speech would have been impossible.

Slowly he came around the coffee table and stood before her. There in the gathering dusk she sensed the warmth radiating from his body, smelled the fresh, clean, soapy smell of him, the faint but unmistakable scent of his aftershave — fruits and spices and a strong but subtle man-smell — and the sensation made her feel even more lightheaded.

She could have retreated had she so desired, or she could have pushed him away or asked him not to do what she knew he was about to do. She did nothing of the kind, however, just stood there and let him reach forward, take her in his arms and pull her gently towards him. She went compliantly, willingly, eager almost, a whirlpool of emotions and desires surfacing within her for the first time as she was carried away on this wonderful tide of discovery.

He bent slightly, bringing his face down toward hers. His long fingers flexed gently, making her tingle from tip to toe, one palm pressed to the small of her back, the other just touching the nape of her neck beneath the dark-blonde spill of her hair.

They kissed.

It was a gentle brushing of lips to begin with, not one long kiss but a series of little meetings and partings, meetings and partings, exploratory at first, as each one bathed in the warmth and the smell and the soft feel of the other. Then, gradually, as he pulled her even closer and she responded in kind, it became insistent, hungrier, more filled with desire. At that moment, each of them could happily have drowned in the embrace of the other.

The moment was timeless. There was no sound in the room other than their own uneven, excited breathing. When at last they broke apart it was with considerable regret, but at the same time each of them was curiously reluctant to look the other in the face.

"I'm sorry for behaving the way I did just now," he said in a low, tender voice. "But when I read your feature and realised you must have actually gone *into* that den of thieves . . . " He let the sentence hang a moment before adding, "God, if anything had happened to you . . . "

She thought she understood his concern now and nodded, still not trusting herself to speak. She looked up into his handsome face. It was obscured by grey shadow now, but very serious. She saw the faint working of his jaw muscles.

Then they kissed again, and this time she felt such a surge of longing that she was more insistent, and possessed of a hitherto undreamed-of desire for him. She pulled him close, so that their two bodies seemed to melt into one, and it was then, in that instant before she gave herself to him completely, that she knew a sudden moment of doubt that led swiftly to panic.

She began to question their actions and motives. After all, could it really be that he felt about her the same way she felt about him? Surely that was expecting too much? Perhaps, then, she was just cheapening herself, allowing him to take advantage of her because he was her employer, and the only real male friend she had so far made in Hong Kong?

It was an unpalatable thought, but persistent, too, and he felt the sudden stiffening of her body beneath his hands just a moment before the thick silence was shattered by the sharp, distracting buzz of the doorbell.

They sprang apart like guilty school-children, all intimacy gone now, replaced by the stiff, guarded formality for which the British are renowned and occasionally ridiculed. Her hands fussing quickly with her hair, she said, "Uh . . . excuse me . . . "

He nodded and mumbled something.

She hurried from the room, both grateful for the intrusion and faintly resentful of it, too. When she opened the door, she found a small, portly Oriental man standing there. He was in his early sixties, with a bullet-head stubbled by a severe crew-cut. It took a moment before she recognised him as the occupant of the flat next door.

"Uh, good evening," she greeted politely, as was the Chinese custom. "Can I help you?"

He was a little surprised by her fluent Chinese, but relieved too, for his own command of English was non-existent. "You are all right?" he asked. "I heard raised voices just now, and then it went very quiet." The old man's rheumy eyes shifted a little so that he could look over her shoulder. In the darkness he could see very little.

She forced a smile. "I'm fine, thank you," she replied. "I'm sorry if I disturbed you."

He stood there a moment longer, then returned his gaze to her face. "As long as you're all right . . . "

"Yes, I am. *M goi*."

He turned away and she closed the door.

She wasn't sure exactly how she felt in that moment. Astonished that she and David had known such intimacy. Disappointed that the moment had not evolved into something even more wonderful. But all of this was so new to her. What did she know about romance? She'd had neither the time nor the inclination for it before this. And that worried her. Dare she give her heart to the first man to affect her in such a strange way, or should she guard herself against possible heartache and humiliation?

She went back into the living-room just as he snapped on the light. At once the room was bathed in a bright, white-yellow glow. She glanced briefly up into his face, knowing the embarrassment now that she had been happy to disregard mere moments before. His expression was unreadable, his lips, so soft before, now drawn into a hard, narrow line. She crossed the room and drew the side-curtains, more for something to do than anything else.

"Can I . . . Would you like a drink or something?" she asked without turning around.

He shook his head, and then, because he realised she couldn't see him, added, "No thanks. I think I'd better go. Lauren, I . . . "

She turned then, her expression as unreadable as his own. "Yes?"

He drew in a deep breath and expelled it as a soft, shuddery kind of sigh. "I'm sorry, Lauren. About just now. I had no right . . . " He shook his head.

"I didn't have to respond," she remarked. "Nobody forced me."

"I know, but . . . " He searched frantically for the right words but in the end only came up with another apology. "I *am* sorry. I mean . . . we've built up a good working relationship over the past week or so. I wouldn't want to ruin that. And I certainly wouldn't want you to think that I tried to take advantage of you here tonight. All I can hope is that you'll overlook my behaviour. I won't let it happen again, I promise."

She wasn't sure whether to be happy or sad about that, and watched him stand there feeling wretched and probably as confused by the turn events had taken as she was herself. He mumbled a goodnight, then turned and hurried from the room. A moment later she heard the front door close softly behind him.

★ ★ ★

Suddenly the weekend had turned into something unhappy and endless, the little flat itself so big and rambling without Maggie there to fill it with good cheer. Lauren slept fitfully that night, distressed by the way David Kent's visit had turned out, and the following morning she set off early to visit the shops, determined to keep her mind occupied with other, less personal concerns. It was, after all, better to be out and about than stuck indoors with her restless emotions.

She returned to The Landmark, where she window-shopped the morning away. She spent the sultry afternoon at the Yub Tai Choon Gallery, admiring the fine works of Chinese art on display there. At the end of the day, however, she had no choice but to return to the empty flat and her troubled thoughts.

Try as she might, those thoughts continued to be dominated by David. She wondered if he had planned any of what had happened at the flat the previous night. Had the emotions he displayed been genuine or merely a facade designed to pierce whatever invisible barriers she may have erected, or was he as surprised by their embrace, and the barely-controlled passion of it, as she had been?

He had spoken briefly of their working relationship. Did he really value that so much that he did not want to jeopardise it by allowing a far more personal bond to take over? Or was that just an excuse, designed perhaps to spare her feelings because he had sensed the sudden cooling of her ardour?

Or were his motives more personal? He was a bachelor, probably already set in the ways of his presumably solitary life. Could it be that he had surrendered to a whim, a moment of weakness inspired by the intimacy of the setting, and then suddenly returned to his senses, possibly after some of her own fears and doubts had communicated themselves to him?

There were so many considerations

that she just couldn't say. And perhaps in later years she would look back on this unsettled time and realise that perhaps that was just as well.

Still . . .

Her bleak mood lifted a little when Maggie returned home early on Sunday evening, full of news about her family, her fiance and her neighbours. It was a welcome relief to share tea and gossip with a friend, and as she sat there at the kitchen table, listening with genuine interest, Lauren once again resolved to put whatever feelings she might have for the *Ex-Pat* editor firmly behind her and just get on with her life.

At last Maggie turned the conversation around to her. "And how was *your* weekend?" she asked. "Did you enjoy having the flat all to yourself?"

"Well, it was certainly peaceful," Lauren said, smiling. "Am I really that noisy?"

"No. To be honest, I missed you, Maggie."

"I am glad. That means we are good

flat-mates." As they drank, Maggie sobered, studying her friend over the rim of her cup. "Lau-ren?" she asked tentatively after a while.

"Hmmm?"

"Is anything *wrong*?" Maggie asked quietly. "You seem . . . upset about something?"

"Upset?"

"Agitated. Dismayed. Sad. Troubled," Maggie replied quite seriously. Her voice grew soft and understanding as she added, "And I think I can probably guess why."

Lauren was surprised, and just a bit embarrassed. Was it really that obvious? But all she said was a very casual, "Oh?"

Maggie nodded sagely. "You are homesick. Yes? You miss your family, friends and country?"

Lauren relaxed slightly. For a moment there . . . But the Chinese girl was not entirely wrong. Lauren *had* known a few odd moments when she had longed to be back home, where life, though quite dull in comparison, had at least been more settled. And at those times, when her spirits had been at their lowest, all her other problems had probably been magnified out of all proportion. It was easier to agree with Maggie's diagnosis than confess the true reasons for her disquiet, though.

"Then it is settled," the Chinese girl announced suddenly.

Lauren eyed her in puzzlement. "What's settled?"

"Next weekend you are coming home with me."

"Oh, no, I — "

"Please. I would like to show off my English friend, and I know my family would like to meet you."

"But — "

Maggie shook her head adamantly. She would not take no for an answer, and so Lauren had little choice but to acquiesce. "All right — so long as it's no bother."

"Of course it is no bother," Maggie assured her.

Lauren smiled for the first time in an age. "Then thank you, Maggie. I shall look forward to it."

The following morning she rose bright and early and caught the tram into work with apprehension tingling in her tummy. How should she behave in front of David? Carry on as normal? Pretend that nothing had happened between them?

Whichever course she took, the situation was certain to be embarrassing. She could only hope that the embarrassment would not last for long.

By the time she alighted from the tram and began the short walk through the Central District to the dingy block from which *The Ex-Pat* was published, she had decided to follow whatever lead David Kent himself elected to take.

She was grateful for the fact that two of her colleagues were already hard at work at their desks by the time she reached the office. She had not relished the prospect of being alone with David again, at least not yet.

Almost as soon as she had finished organising her work-schedule for the morning, however, David came out of his office and asked if he could have a word.

At once Lauren felt the butterflies in her tummy come fluttering back to life. But perhaps it was as well to have this business out once and for all, clear the air, so to speak, and confirm exactly where each of them stood with the other, and as she followed him back into his office, she was preparing herself to do exactly that.

David evidently had something else to discuss with her, however, and as he gestured that she should take a seat, she realised that he was behaving exactly as if nothing had happened between them, as if he wanted quite desperately to carry on as normal and put the entire episode behind him.

"How was your weekend?" he asked politely.

Previously-suppressed bitterness suddenly surfaced within her, entirely without warning. "How do you think?" she countered before she could stop herself.

She regretted taking such a tone immediately. It would do nothing to improve an already-strained atmosphere. But the words were already out; it was too late to offer a more perfunctory reply.

He looked into her face, his own rugged countenance tired and vaguely sad. He nodded slowly, accepting her statement with the resignation of one who knows the impossibility of trying to undo damage already wrought. He cleared his throat. "Silly question," he said quietly.

She hated herself in that moment, though quite why, she couldn't say. "You forgot to take my piece on illegal dentists with you when you left on Friday evening," she said, making an effort to sound more casual. "I brought it in with me again this morning."

"Thanks. I . . . " He broke off and made a gesture of frustration.

He had no time for this charade, she realised. He was too genuine for that. "Look," he said, dropping his careful but deliberate politeness, "I meant what I said, Lauren. It was a wonderful piece, and I *do* intend to use it. But I also meant what I said about taking unnecessary risks. No more investigative journalism unless I say so, all right?"

She shrugged. "I suppose."

He looked across the desk at her. Regret was plain in his eyes for just an instant, but regret for what? That their relationship had become so formal? That it had not developed as he had hoped?

Then the emotion was gone and he was once again the busy editor. "Now, tell me — what do you know about Ricky Lee?"

She ran the name through her mind. "Nothing," she replied at length.

"Well, we're going to have to change that — fast."

"Why? Who is he?"

"Probably the biggest movie star Hong Kong's produced in the last ten years."

"But I've never heard of him."

"You wouldn't have. He's big, but he hasn't quite made it as an international star yet, although he's unquestionably the biggest box-office draw in Asia — and with some justification.

"About three years ago, the Silver Crop Studio up near Mount Cameron looked almost certain to close down. They'd produced one unsuccessful movie after another, and their finances were practically at rock bottom. Then they released a film starring Ricky Lee and it turned out to be one of the biggest-grossing Chinese films of all time. Since then he's been the jewel in Silver Crop's crown."

As direct as ever, Lauren said, "And what has all this got to do with me?"

"Silver Crop have arranged for Ricky to give a rare but exclusive interview — to *The Ex-Pat*."

Suddenly realisation began to dawn,

and as she understood exactly what he was leading up to, the journalist in her took over completely. "And you want *me* to conduct the interview?"

He nodded. "Yes. If you'd like to try it."

"Do you think I could?"

"I wouldn't have assigned it to you if I didn't think you could handle it."

Lauren sat back, thinking about it. It was the most marvellous news she could have wished for, especially after the weekend she had just experienced, but more than that, it was a chance to really make her mark.

"When is the interview to take place?"

"At the studio, ten o'clock tomorrow morning."

"Do we have any file clippings on this fellow?" she asked. "I'll have to do my research before I can formulate my questions."

"I've already dug out everything we've got. The studio's also supplied a potted biography and filmography, too."

He handed a folder across to her, and in her eagerness to take it, their fingertips touched briefly. For a second or two she came back down to earth with a jolt. Even that casual contact had made her tingle, and remember exactly the feelings she had known in his embrace the previous Friday night.

"Thank you," she said in a subdued voice. "I . . . I'll read through all of this tonight."

"You'd better. The studio will be sending a limousine to pick you up from your apartment at nine o'clock tomorrow morning."

They both stood up, some — though not all — of the awkwardness between them now dispelled. "Good luck, Lauren," he said, treating her to a brief, wistful smile. "I know you won't let us down."

5

Lauren studied herself critically in the full-length mirror in Maggie's bedroom one last time. Behind her, the bright, saffron-coloured sunshine of Tuesday morning filtered in through the curtains to backlight her appealingly. She had decided to wear a matching skirt and jacket of the palest green for her meeting with Ricky Lee. A smart, open-necked blouse set off the outfit.

"Well?" asked Maggie, from the doorway.

Lauren smiled uncertainly. She hadn't expected to be quite as nervous as this. After all, nerves were for amateurs, and she was a professional. But the more she'd thought about it, the more she had come to appreciate the true enormity of this assignment.

Ricky Lee rarely gave interviews. It was evidently all part of his mystique, and meant that whoever had the opportunity to question him only had one chance to get it right. It was an awesome responsibility for a girl who took her job so seriously, and that knowledge did little to help calm her nerves.

"Lau-ren?" prompted Maggie. "You are all right?"

She nodded. "Yes, fine, thanks."

At precisely nine o'clock, the doorbell rang and Lauren exchanged a loaded glance with Maggie. "Well," said the blonde girl. "This is it, I suppose. Wish me luck."

"Of course," smiled Maggie, raising both hands to show that she had her fingers crossed.

Lauren quickly checked inside her shoulder-bag to make certain that everything was there. Miniature tape recorder, note-pad, two pens, a brief guide to the questions she intended to ask Ricky Lee.

She swung the bag up onto her shoulder and hurried to answer the door. Out in the tiled, softly-lit hallway stood a very erect Oriental in his late twenties. He was immaculately attired in a creaseless grey chauffeur's uniform, and held a peaked cap across the two rows of shiny gold buttons that ran up over his chest.

"Miss Adams?" he asked in a quiet, polite tone.

"Yes."

"I am from the studio," he said, his English slow but very precise. He produced an identity card which confirmed his position at Silver Crop. "You are ready to go?"

"Yes, of course."

He escorted her across to the elevator, at great pains to make sure that even the most mundane task, such as pushing the button to call the lift, was spared her. On the way down to the underground car-park, she broke the silence by asking him how far the studio was.

"Not far, miss. Half an hour, if the traffic is with us."

He said no more, though. He had doubtless been trained to view his position as a lowly one, and would have considered any attempt to instigate a conversation with his passenger unforgivable.

The lift came to a halt, and as they stepped out into the underground car-park, Lauren found herself confronted with a gleaming silver Rolls-Royce. The chauffeur hurried forward to open one of the rear doors for her, and she nodded her thanks as she climbed inside.

The interior was comfort itself. The cool air was discreetly conditioned. The seat was upholstered in such a way as to mould itself to the passenger's body. There was a miniature drinks cabinet, even a television, video and CD player.

The chauffeur settled himself behind the steering wheel and started the engine. A moment later, the car purred softly out onto the expressway.

Lauren could hardly believe all of this

was happening. It was just too good to be true. But she was determined not to let it all go to her head. She was going to do the best job she possibly could. She had read all of the biographical material the studio had supplied and gone through all the clippings David Kent had managed to find. But the emphasis was always on Ricky Lee the movie star, never Ricky Lee the man, and it was this angle that she intended to pursue. Why was he so successful? What made him tick? Was there a special woman behind him? These were the questions she wanted to ask, the questions that would make *her* feature the definitive one.

As Hong Kong flew past beyond the tinted windows, she thought back to the previous day. Once David had given her the assignment, her mood had lightened considerably. Now she had something other than the *Ex-Pat* editor to occupy her mind. David had given her an important task, though, and she hoped that his decision had been based on her merits as a writer, and not out of some misguided desire to make up for his behaviour the previous Friday night. It was only when she reached home that evening and told Maggie the news that she began to realise just how important an assignment it really was, though.

"Ricky *Lee*?" Maggie's large brown eyes had grown even wider. "*Really*?"

"Really," Lauren replied casually.

"You are not pulling my arm?"

"Leg," Lauren corrected with a laugh. "And no — I'm not pulling it."

Maggie regarded her in awe. "Oh, how lucky you are. I have friends back home who would sell their souls for the opportunity you have now!"

"But he's only an actor," Lauren pointed out.

Maggie looked positively offended. "Only?" she echoed. "No, Lau-ren. He is much more. He is a film star."

Lauren was still unable to grasp the nature of the man's appeal, though.

"What is it that makes him so special, then?" she asked, genuinely interested.

"I cannot explain," Maggie replied. "It is difficult to put into words. It is probably easier to show you."

"*Show* me?"

Maggie nodded and offered her another of her infectious grins. "Yes. Come along, we are going out."

"Where?"

"To see Ricky's latest film."

"But I've only just come in!"

"No problem. We can get something to eat on the way!"

And that was how Lauren first encountered Ricky Lee, on a cinema screen sixty feet high and one hundred feet wide, in a darkened cinema that was packed with but a small fraction of Ricky Lee's most ardent admirers, mostly young girls in their late teens, but also many older women.

The film was a costume drama, a little too stilted for Lauren's Western tastes, but certainly something of a spectacular. Ricky played a warlord whose love for the daughter of his arch-rival brings about a fierce battle. In the final scenes, after his love had been killed in one of the film's many skirmishes, Ricky realises that he must commit suicide in order to stop his enemies from completely destroying his kingdom.

It was all very melodramatic, but there could be no doubting Ricky's abilities as an actor. He dominated every scene he was in, and he imbued his character with strength and dignity without having to resort to the posturing of many of his co-stars. Even though she couldn't quite keep up with some of the Chinese dialogue, Lauren was able to follow most of the story, and during Ricky's final scenes, even she had to blink away a few sudden tears.

Now, as they left the city behind them and followed a winding road that led ever higher through forested slopes, she concluded that it had been a useful introduction to the man she was about to interview, and she could understand a little better now why he was the biggest star in Asia.

Just over half an hour later she caught sight of the studio gates up ahead, and felt a thrill of anticipation run through her. After a brief stop at the gatehouse, where a security man waved them through after exchanging a few words with the chauffeur, the Rolls-Royce ferried them across to the studio's administrative offices. Here she was greeted by a publicity woman who introduced herself as Nora Chow.

"Ah, Miss Adams. I am so glad you could make it."

"Believe me, there was no way I was going to miss it."

Nora Chow nodded her understanding. "Yes, Ricky does not give interviews all that often. In fact, he is waiting for you now on Lot Three, where we are shooting his new film. Do you need to freshen up at all?"

"No, I'm fine, thanks."

"Then I will take you across to meet him."

It was a short walk, through large hangar-like structures which served as sound-stages, and then past some impressive standing sets which included pagodas, castle walls, ornamental gardens and the like.

Glancing around, Lauren began to soak up some of the feel of the studio. It was a veritable hive of activity. About a hundred yards straight ahead she saw a crowd of technicians congregating around a car that was brightly illuminated by several arc lamps. Before they could reach it, however, Nora Chow led them around a corner, and it was then that Lauren saw Ricky Lee in the flesh for the first time, sprawled out in a canvas chair, legs crossed at the ankles, resting his chin on one fist and holding a script in the other. A second chair had been set up across from him, as well as a little table upon which had been left a bright red Cool Bag. When they were near enough, Nora Chow called Ricky by name, and he sat up and turned a little to face them.

As soon as he saw Lauren, he jumped to his feet, dropped his script onto the table and came forward to meet her with one hand outstretched. He was quite tall for an Oriental, Lauren saw; at five feet ten inches, he was just a couple of inches taller than she herself. He took her hand in his. His grip was gentle and cool, and when he said, "Hi, there. It's Lauren, isn't it? From *The Ex-Pat*?", he looked directly into her face with eyes that were so dark they were very nearly black, though well-spaced and quite open.

"Good morning, Mr Lee. I'm very pleased to meet you."

"The feeling's mutual," he responded with effortless charm. "But Mr Lee was my father; I answer best to plain Ricky."

She dipped her head, somewhat reassured by his relaxed manner. "Ricky it is, then."

Nora Chow excused herself once the introductions had been made, and as she turned and walked away, Ricky Lee gestured that Lauren should take the seat across from him, which she did.

Ricky was, like herself, in his mid-twenties, and although he had a boyish face, his classical looks held about them something that was at once both youthful and mature. His hair was as completely blue-black as midnight. He wore it at medium-length, and without a parting. His pale, narrow lips showed good humour. He appeared slim and graceful beneath his tight-fitting T-shirt and designer jeans, but muscular, too. He had a marvellous bronze cast to his skin.

Lauren unzipped her shoulder-bag and took out her note-pad and miniature tape-recorder. Although she'd thought she was suffering from nerves earlier on, that was nothing to how she felt now that she was actually face to face with the film star. Perhaps it would have been easier had she not seen him at the cinema first, but it was too late for that now; she must overcome her anxiety and do as professional a job as possible.

He must have realised that she was a little nervous, because he indicated the Cool Bag on the table beside him. "Can I get you a soft drink?" he asked, his English betraying a very faint American accent.

Lauren smiled and nodded. "Thank you."

He took two ice-cold Cokes from the bag and passed one across to her. "Now," he said. "You're in luck. This is one of the very few days that the studio has decided it can do without me, so I'm entirely at your disposal. Ask me whatever you want, and I'll do my best to answer you as honestly as I can."

"Your English is very good," she said.'

"That's because my parents moved to Australia when I was about two years old. I lived there until I was ten, and then they sent me back here and enrolled me at the China Drama Academy."

"The China Drama Academy?" she repeated with a frown. "Is that a kind of stage school?"

"Yes. But it's not like any stage school you might have in England. Oh, you're taught to act, sing, dance and so on, sure. But you also have to learn gymnastics, acrobatics and martial arts."

"It all sounds very strenuous."

He laughed at that. "To give you some idea just *how* strenuous, it's written into your contract that if you die during your training, the school is completely absolved of all blame."

She sipped her drink, beginning to feel a little more like normal. He was so willing to talk, and so casual about his superstar status, that he automatically put her at ease.

The morning flew by. Ricky was a born raconteur, and she found him fascinating. He was patient, polite, considerate and he appeared to be totally unspoiled by his success. He spoke lovingly of the Hollywood movies upon which he had grown up, passionately about his work now, and was quite candid when Lauren asked him what had prompted him to break his customary silence and grant this rare interview.

"I'm a movie star," he said. "But I'm only a movie star in Asia. Now, I think, the time is right to broaden my appeal."

She smiled mischievously. "Ah, I see. So this interview is really intended to help introduce you to us *gwailos*."

He smiled at her use of the derogatory term for Caucasians, or 'foreign devils'. "That's right. But it's not quite as mercenary as that. Exposure helps to promote my films at home, too."

"Well, I'll certainly see what I can do to help you in that regard," she promised.

He frowned. "That sounds as if the interview is over."

"Well, I suppose it is," she replied.

Glancing at her watch, she was surprised to see that they had in fact been chatting — it had all been too informal to call it an interview — for more than three hours. "In any case, I'm sure I've taken up far more of your time than I meant to."

"The pleasure was all mine, I assure you," he said gallantly. As she began to gather up her things, he added, "I'll tell you what; why don't we continue the interview over lunch?"

"Oh, I couldn't — "

"Why not? Oh, I know — it's the food you're worried about, isn't it? The studio canteen *does* have a reputation, I know. But the rumours are totally groundless, I promise you."

She laughed. "No, it's not that."

"You think I might slap you with the bill afterwards?" he asked teasingly, raising one fine eyebrow.

She decided to match his light banter. "Well, it had crossed my mind . . . "

"No, come on, I'm serious," he said, sitting forward. "I have no other commitments today, and I'm certain that you haven't got to rush back to your newspaper right away."

Lauren held back for a moment longer. She was flattered by his invitation, and also by his insistence that she accept. And she did find him entertaining company. He had such drive and ambition, and yet he did not take himself seriously. And it was the kind of opportunity that would not present itself every day. "All right, then, Ricky. Thank you."

"Thank *you*," he countered.

They walked side by side across to the studio carpark, where Ricky opened the passenger-side door of his bright red, open-topped sports car and indicated that she should climb in. He settled himself comfortably beside her, gunned the powerful engine and drove them out of the studio and back towards the city.

As the warm breeze ran its intangible fingers through her dark-blonde hair, Lauren had to pinch herself to make sure she wasn't dreaming. To have been given the chance to interview a famous film star was one thing, but to then be taken to lunch by him . . . !

He took them to an exclusive restaurant in the Happy Valley area of the island, where he was evidently well-known, and they dined on an array of spicy Szechuan food. The interview continued in an even more informal manner as he instructed her on the correct way of using chopsticks. He explained his philosophy of acting, his reaction to his critics, his forthcoming movie. As far as his private life was concerned, he had always been too busy for personal relationships, and in any case, the only people he knew really well were film people, and by and large he found them to be rather shallow and superficial.

After lunch he insisted that she see some of the island with him, but she protested that she really ought to get back to the office. "Oh, come on," he implored with a boyish kind of enthusiasm she found difficult to resist. "Believe me, your office isn't going anywhere."

"Well . . . "

The afternoon — simply spent sightseeing — was wonderful. Towards the end of it, he drove them to an area known as Lover's Peak, on Bowen Road.

"According to the legend," he explained, "a woman was told to come here to pray after her lover died, and when she did, her prayers were answered. Ever since then, women who seek good luck in love come here to pray as she did."

A few women were already there, standing quietly here and there in meditation or introspection.

Seeing them, Ricky frowned. "What's today's date, Lauren?"

"The sixteenth."

"Ah, that explains it."

"Explains what?"

"Today's date. It has a six in it. That

means it is a good day to come and ask for luck in love."

The next time she checked her wristwatch, Lauren was startled to see that the afternoon had vanished and early evening was approaching. "Good heavens!" she said. "I must get back!"

"If you must," he replied with what appeared to be genuine regret.

"I must, I'm afraid."

"You have enjoyed yourself, though?"

"Very much. But I don't get paid to enjoy myself, Ricky."

"Relax," he said easily. "If you're worried about getting into trouble with your boss, I'll square things for you. You're giving him an exclusive, don't forget. He should promote you for that."

But he sensed that she wouldn't be happy until she had at least phoned her office, so he suggested they find a call-box. When she made the call, however, there was no reply. It was the end of the working day, and everyone must have gone home.

As she replaced the handset, Ricky asked her if she would like to go on to a nightclub, but this time she insisted that, as much as she enjoyed his company, she really must get home. He acquiesced graciously and drove her swiftly back through the city to her apartment. They reached their destination just as the sun began to sink in the west and the sky over Hong Kong turned a very pale turquoise.

When he switched off the engine, silence settled over the deserted underground car-park. He twisted around to face her, his classically handsome face bathed in the soft saffron glow of the overhead lights.

"Thank you for a wonderful day, Ricky," she said with a smile.

"I hope you enjoyed it as much as I did."

"Oh, I did. I never dreamed . . . well, what I mean is, when I woke up this morning, I thought I would interview you and that would be that. But you've been so kind to me, and so generous with your time."

He reached over to place one palm lightly on her shoulder, and his touch thrilled her. "Believe me," he said. "It's I who should thank you. It's not often I get the chance to spend time with a *real* person." He nodded in the direction of the lift. "Shall I see you to your flat?"

Lauren considered that. It seemed to be an innocuous enough suggestion, and yet she wondered if there were something more behind his offer? Perhaps it was just her imagination, giving his words a suggestive emphasis he had not intended.

"That's all right, thanks all the same," she replied lightly, adding by way of explanation, "My flat-mate is one of your biggest fans. I don't know that she would get over the shock if you were to suddenly turn up on her doorstep."

He grinned. "Maybe next time, then."

The possibility of there *being* a next time — a fact Lauren herself had not even considered — filled her with excitement. But as she climbed out of the car and waved once to Ricky before stepping into the lift, she cautioned herself against getting too carried away. He was doubtless just being polite. After all, he was a movie star. He could have his pick of women. What made her believe that she was so special that he would wish to see her again?

6

The very next day, Wednesday, Lauren and Maggie travelled into work together.

Lauren found it hard to settle down to the normal office routine after all the excitement of the previous day, but at least she was able to relive some of its magic while she transcribed everything that Ricky had said and began to organise it into some sort of logical order.

In a way, however, writing the feature only served to reinforce Ricky's star status, a status that rendered him largely unapproachable to her. She realised that she had been foolish to allow him to captivate her with his very special charm, that he had only behaved as personably as he had in order to ensure that her article reflected favourably on him. Still, if that were the case, he needn't have worried. How could she have painted an unflattering picture of him, when there was nothing unflattering to say about him?

Around mid-morning, David Kent came out of his office and crossed over to see how she was getting on. She was apparently so engrossed in her work that she didn't even know he was there at first.

"So," he said, smiling down at her. "How did it go yesterday, with the great man himself?"

She looked up with a start, realising that she'd been daydreaming. "Oh, David!" Quickly she gathered her wits, still as unable to put the memory of their embrace completely from her mind as she was to totally resist his easy-going, pleasant manner. "Ah . . . yes. It was . . . a very interesting experience. But I'm terribly sorry I wasn't able to get back to the office — "

"Oh, don't worry about that. I didn't really expect you back. But did you get enough material for the feature?"

"More than enough."

"Maybe we should serialise it over two issues, then," he suggested.

"See what you think when you read it," she replied. "With any luck I'll have it on your desk by five o'clock."

"I'll look forward to it."

He was just about to stand up and go when the phone on her desk rang. She answered it promptly and said into the mouthpiece, "Hello?"

A woman at the other end of the line said, "Ah, good morning. Is that Miss Adams speaking?"

"Yes. Can I help you?"

"I am Angela Yuen, Ricky Lee's secretary."

"Oh!"

David had been about to leave her to talk in private. Now her startled exclamation made him pause, to ensure that everything was all right.

"I have a call for you from Mr Lee," said the woman at the other end of the line. "Connecting you now."

There was a click and then Ricky's

voice came clearly into Lauren's ear. "Hello, Lauren?"

"Ricky. How . . . how nice to hear from you again. What can I do for you?"

"Well, you can say yes."

"To what?"

"A little informal gathering here at the studio tonight. We're going to look at a rough-cut of some scenes from my new film, the producers, the director, the money-men and myself, then have a meal afterwards."

Again Lauren had difficulty in believing that all this was actually happening to her. "And you want me to accompany you?"

"Well, I was hoping that you might persuade your maiden aunt to go with me," he replied with a chuckle. "Of course I want you to accompany me!"

"Well, I'm not sure . . . "

"Look, I have to dash — I'm wanted back on the set. I'll send a car for you at around seven, all right?"

"But — "

"'Bye."

The line went dead.

Lauren sat there, holding the handset to her ear. She was stunned. She had not thought to hear from him again. And yet he had taken time out from a hectic schedule just to ask her to accompany him to some sort of studio soiree . . . Again she was flattered by his attentions.

"Lauren?"

She looked up. David was studying her with concern.

"Is everything all right?"

She smiled and put the phone down at last. "Yes. At least, I think so."

"You don't sound very sure."

"That was Ricky Lee on the phone," she explained. "He . . . he wants me to attend a screening of his new film tonight."

David took the news with a neutral expression, though it was easy to see that it did not exactly meet with his approval. After a very long time, however, he finally nodded. "You obviously made an impression on him," he said quietly. "Are you going?"

Her laugh betrayed her embarrassment. "He really didn't leave me much choice."

"It should be quite an experience," he said politely. "I hope you enjoy it."

She watched him walk away, her sense of euphoria somehow spoiled by an irrational but nonetheless powerful feeling that she had betrayed him in some way.

The feeling persisted right through the remainder of the day, though why she should feel so troubled remained a mystery to her. After all, she and David meant nothing to each other. He had, in fact, made that abundantly clear. Theirs was a professional relationship. That had been his choice. And yet she could not stop thinking that she was somehow being disloyal to him.

At last the working day began to wind to a close, and one by one her colleagues rose from their desks, called their goodnights and headed for the elevator. Lauren, engrossed in her work, barely looked up. So preoccupied had she been all day that she had found it increasingly difficult to concentrate on the job at hand. Sentences would not form themselves coherently in her mind. Every attempt to type out a fresh paragraph would inevitably result in her making at least two errors.

"Lau-ren?"

She glanced up to see Maggie standing before her desk, her expression expectant. "You are coming home now?" the pretty Chinese girl asked.

"In a little while. I want to finish this first."

"But you have to get ready for your date tonight," Maggie reminded her.

"Oh, that won't take long."

Maggie indicated the papers spread across her desk. "Can this not wait?"

"It could, but I'd as soon get it finished and on David's desk."

"Shall I wait for you, then?"

"No. I'm not sure how long I'll be

yet, and the last thing I want to do is keep you hanging around."

Maggie nodded her understanding. "Very well. I will see you back at the flat later, then."

Left alone, Lauren continued to beaver away until at last she had produced a sheaf of neatly-typed pages. She quickly read through them one last time, making small corrections with a blue pencil, and then tapped the whole thing into shape and took it through to David's office.

He was also working late. He looked up as she came through the door, and put his pen down in order to run his fingers up through his blue-black hair and stretch his spine.

"The Ricky Lee interview," she said, handing it over.

He took it with a nod. "Thanks." Suddenly he frowned and glanced at his wristwatch. "Hey, I didn't mean for you to work late to get it finished."

"Oh, that's all right. I thought I would. You know, to give you enough time to decide exactly how you want to publish it."

He quickly glanced through it. "It all looks pretty good."

"Thank you."

She stood there for a moment longer, again uncertain just what to say or how to behave. She saw from the look on his own face that he shared the sensation too, and she felt vaguely sad that the easiness of their relationship had somehow been replaced by this difficult, frequently embarrassing pretence.

"Well, I suppose I'd better be off, then," she said, attempting to lighten the moment.

"Yes," he said. "You don't want to be late for your date."

"No, quite."

She turned to go, and made it as far as the door before he said — impulsively, so it seemed, "Lauren — take care, won't you."

She turned back to face him. It was such an odd thing for him to say that she could not mask the frown on her forehead. "Of course," she replied cautiously. He was looking at her so earnestly that her puzzlement only intensified. "David," she said carefully, "is there anything wrong?"

"Apart from the obvious?" he replied with a brief, sour smile.

"What do you mean by that?" she asked. She knew exactly what he meant, though. He was referring to the pair of them, the feeling that obviously existed between them, the feeling that had somehow formed a gulf which neither of them seemed able to cross. He shook his head and shrugged all in one movement. "Nothing. Forget it. Just watch out for yourself . . . when you're around Ricky Lee."

Immediately she turned defensive, sensing that he was implying something about Ricky which Ricky himself was currently in no position to refute. "David," she said quietly. "If you've got something to say, perhaps you'd better just say it."

"Even if it hurts you?" he said.

"Who's to say that it *will* hurt?"

"The truth always does," he pointed out cynically.

Already short-tempered — with herself as much as anyone — she lost patience with him. "If you're going to speak in riddles . . . " she began, turning away.

He stood up quickly, dropping her feature onto his desk. "Look," he said sharply. "Perhaps it's none of my business, but it's like I said before. I have a certain responsibility towards you. That's why I'm telling you . . . "

She faced him directly, and a little defiantly. "Yes?"

He tried to choose his words with care. "Watch just how far you allow yourself to become involved with Ricky Lee," he said softly.

Her lips drew tight in anger. "What I do in my private life . . . "

"If you get involved with that man, it won't be long before what happens in your private life affects your professional life, too," he said, coming around the desk.

"Why?"

"Because he has a reputation. A well-earned reputation."

"Oh?"

"Yes. As something of a ladies' man."

She snorted. "That's nonsense."

"And what do you base that on? One day spent chatting to him in a studio?" Again he made a gesture of frustration. There was little about him that was easy-going and relaxed now. He was restless, like a caged tiger. "Look, all I'm telling you is what I know for a fact. It's up to you whether or not you believe me. But the least I can do is forewarn you. The man's a notorious womanizer."

She made to object but he talked her down. "Oh, I know. You think he's squeaky-clean. And so he is — in public. The studio's become very adept at covering up all his little 'indiscretions'. But I promise you, Lauren, he'll blind you with his charm and he'll use you, and when a younger or prettier face comes along, he'll cast you aside so fast that your head will spin."

"How dare you!" she hissed, outraged.

"I dare," he said, "because I *care*."

For a moment she said nothing. In truth, she no longer knew what to believe. But was David telling the truth? She could only go by the evidence of her own experience. So far, Ricky had treated her with nothing but respect.

Before she properly had a chance to think about what she was going to say, she asked, "Do you know what I think, David?"

He shook his head wearily. "No."

"I think you're jealous," she said venomously. "I think you resent the fact that Ricky and I got on so well yesterday, and you're deliberately trying to turn me against him."

His eyes slid away from hers when she said the word *jealous*, and she knew a moment of senseless, idiotic triumph. "I see you were right about one thing, though," she finished unfairly. "The truth *does* hurt."

He crossed the office in three long strides, moving fast, not angry, just determined. He grabbed her by the arms, not hard, but with passion. She looked into his face. Again she could sense the warmth of him, the soapy, scented smell of him, the sudden giddying surge of feeling that she had known during their first, and only, embrace, and she wondered if she were about to relive that magical moment again.

He looked deep into her eyes. She saw a fire smouldering in his own dark orbs. He opened his mouth, whether in preparation for a kiss or to say something, she couldn't tell. But then the electric silence of the moment was shattered as the phone on his desk began to ring.

It rang again and again as they stood there, he with his slim, long-fingered hands encircling her bare arms, his eyes trapping her own in an intense, almost mesmeric stare. Her mouth went dry. She didn't know whether she wanted him to kiss her or not, but she thought deep down that she did, very much.

Then he released her and wheeled away, snatched up the phone and said one word; "Yes?"

She stood there, watching his back. A shiver ran through her as the tension of the moment began to leave her. Then she saw his shoulders straighten, his head snap up. "Where?" he asked into the mouthpiece, his voice urgent. "Damn . . . And how long ago?"

He listened into the phone for a moment longer. Then; "All right. Thanks, Jack — I owe you one."

He put the phone down, snatched his light cotton jacket from where he had draped it across the back of his chair and pulled a camera from one of his desk-drawers.

"What is it?" she asked, her own newswoman's curiosity sensing that a story had just broken.

"You know those crowded tenements

down by the harbour?"

"Yes."

"A fire's broken out there. A *bad* one, by all accounts."

"You're going to cover it?" she asked.

"Uh-huh. Lock up here for me, will you?"

"I'll come with you."

That brought him up sharp. He turned to face her. "What about your date?"

"This is more important," she said, all her previous enmity now gone.

He nodded. "Come on, then."

They both left the office quickly, Lauren stopping only to grab her shoulder-bag, and then they rode the elevator down to the ground floor.

Outside, the early-evening traffic was already fearsome, but David hailed a taxi and told the driver to get them to the scene of the blaze as quickly as he could. As an added inducement to do just that, David stuffed a wad of dollar bills into the man's calloused hand.

As the cab pulled away from the curb and began to follow a seemingly meandering course full of slim little back-streets and 'go-downs' in order to reach its destination, David checked the camera to make sure it was fully loaded and in good working order. His mind was obviously elsewhere, though; with the residents of those mean, overcrowded tenements that lined the harbour-front.

"That was Jack Mason who called," he explained distractedly. "He's one of the area's fire-control officers." He cursed suddenly. "Damn! It was only a matter of time before something like this happened, I guess. You know yourself how dry and hot it's been these last few weeks. Those tenements will be like tinder now."

Lauren shared his concern. On an island so limited in space, hundreds of thousands of less fortunate people lived a mean, cramped existence in one shanty town after another. Each overcrowded block was a fire-trap just waiting to ignite.

As they drew closer to their destination, they began to see evidence of the fire up ahead. Traffic was slowing to a crawl to make way for emergency vehicles. Fire engines, ambulances and police cars blurred past with sirens wailing and lights flashing. Police officers began to set up diversions in order to keep traffic away from the scene of the blaze.

They had slowed to a snail's-pace now, and when David gauged that they were close enough to complete their journey on foot, he reached forward, tapped the driver on the shoulder and said, "You can drop us here."

There was a palpable tension in the early evening air. They felt it as soon as they stepped out onto the pavement. In the distance they heard the rise and fall of one siren blending with the cacophony of another dozen, quite possibly more.

"Come on," said David. He reached

out to take her hand and led her down the crowded street, and even though her adrenalin was pumping madly and her journalist's instincts were at their most acute, she could not ignore the thrill of his touch.

As they approached the intersection, it became obvious that the fire was every bit as bad as David's contact at the fire department had predicted. The emergency services had cordoned off the area with bright yellow tape, and policemen were patrolling the lines to keep order among the muttering onlookers. David shouldered his way through the crowd without breaking stride, holding firmly onto Lauren lest they be separated in all the confusion. When he reached the tape he flashed his identification card, and seeing that he was a member of the press, the officer who hurried across to stop them from going any further, waved them through instead.

The street had been a shambles to begin with, narrow, permanently greyed with the shadows cast by the mean, ramshackle tenements, where the trapped air grew stale, oppressive and stifling. Now, however, with bright red fire engines everywhere, thick hosepipes snaking in every direction across the road and yellow-helmeted firemen racing backwards and forwards to tend one emergency or another, it resembled nothing so much as a scene from the Blitz.

Lauren could not suppress a shudder.

David glanced down at her. "Are you all right?" he asked with concern.

Not trusting herself to speak, she only nodded. About mid-way down the south-facing block, bright amber flames licked greedily at windowsills and balconies. A thick, burgeoning column of black smoke spewed up into the deep blue sky. The roar of the flames dominated every other sound in the street, mingling with and frequently drowning out the fire chief's yelled orders, the wailing of sirens and the shocked, distressed cries and shouts of suddenly homeless men, women and children.

Lauren quickly palmed tears from her own eyes. As much as her heart went out to these people, she was a professional. She was here to cover a story — a horrifying story, certainly — but cover it she must.

"Lauren? Lauren!"

She looked up, startled. "What? I'm sorry, David. What did you just say?"

David had to raise his voice to make himself heard. "I said that I'm going to find Jack Mason and get some background information on this affair. I shouldn't be too long."

"All right."

"Go and stand over there, by that fire-truck. I'll be back as soon as I can."

Lauren did not really want to be alone amidst all of this noise and seeming confusion, but she bobbed her head and he let go of her hand and hurried away. Lauren stood there for a moment, watching him go. Then she took her miniature tape-recorder from her bag and switched it on, intending to dictate her thoughts at that moment.

But her voice had somehow dried up. Seeing all this devastation now, her own concerns seemed so petty and insignificant. Her job, too . . .

Suddenly everything seemed to fall into perspective. What was more important — helping these poor people, or standing idly by to dictate an eye-witness account of the blaze for her readers to scan over a calm and unhurried breakfast the following week? She stuffed the tape-recorder back into her bag. She did not even have to think about the answer.

She moved around the fire-truck. About seventy or eighty feet away, three smudge-faced firemen were shepherding a column of dazed and shuffling residents from one smouldering building, even as another crew raised a hose and directed a jet of water at the charring walls, where it splashed and hissed and appeared to bounce back off the grey wood and concrete in a white spray.

Her attention returned to the firemen who were guiding their charges across to a waiting rank of ambulances. They looked exhausted, all three of them, as they loosened their breathing apparatus to offer words of encouragement or direction to the bewildered and now displaced residents, many of whom were clutching the few pitiful remnants they had managed to salvage from their burning homes at the very last minute.

Another fireman raced across to them. Lauren heard him quite clearly as he raised his voice. "Did you get everyone out?"

The first of the firemen nodded. "That's the lot," he confirmed.

Lauren felt herself go a little light-headed. Thank goodness for that — ! But even as her eyes travelled back up towards the building, the breath caught in her throat. She could have sworn she'd seen a face at one of those dark, soulless first-floor windows; small, round, scared . . . a child's face, filled with despair, his cheeks shining with spilled tears.

She was so startled that she had to reach out and grab the edge of the fire-truck to maintain her balance. The next time she looked up at the building, however, the window in question was as empty and devoid of life as it had been before.

Lauren told herself that she must have been imagining it. After all, hadn't she just this minute heard the firemen confirm that the building had been completely evacuated? But she could hardly doubt the evidence of her own eyes, as fleeting as it had been. At least one person was left in that raging inferno, a totally helpless little boy.

Lauren had to tell the three firemen. She began to hurry towards them, but before she could attract their attention, another official called to them and they rushed away from her.

She slowed down. As she watched

the firemen surge away to help fight a fire that had broken out in another part of the block, her feeling of loneliness and isolation increased. She glanced around, searching for someone else to tell. Everywhere she looked, she saw firemen busy with one task or another. She tried to find David, but smoke stretched across the narrow street in thick grey wreaths, and he was nowhere to be seen.

Her feeling of utter helplessness was frustrating, but more important was the fact that the little boy trapped in the burning tenement was running out of time.

Quickly she made a decision, and before she could change her mind, she hurried towards the building.

She went inside.

At once darkness swallowed her whole. She knew a brief, unpleasant moment of sheer, blind panic, but forced it down by an effort of will so intense that it left her feeling giddy. She tried to breathe in. Immediately she tasted acrid smoke on her tongue. She took a handkerchief from her bag, flicked it open and held it across her lower face. Then she went deeper into the building.

She heard flames licking hungrily at the timbers far above her. Their roaring was constant and all consuming. Water being directed onto the inferno from outside immediately turned to steam upon contact with the flames, and its reptilian hiss did nothing to quieten her fears. Here and there escaping water trickled down the stairwell like molten silver.

Lauren was rooted to the spot momentarily, trying to get her bearings before daring to move any deeper into the structure. Visibility was poor. Smoke was drifting around her ankles. But she must not risk getting herself lost. Her own life, as well as that of the child she was hoping to rescue, depended upon her being able to find her way back down to this exit.

At last she went deeper along the

dingy hallway. She found the foot of the rickety staircase on her left, turned and began to climb, testing each stair before putting her full weight on it.

Cautiously, she continued her ascent.

7

The burning tenement had become a world of its own, a dark, foul-smelling world with smoke for an atmosphere and the shifting, uncertain orange-yellow glow of dancing flames for daylight. It seemed hard to believe that so much was going on in the street outside to end this blaze, because the flames eating the building made such noise that nothing could be heard of the men outside.

Lauren raised one foot in preparation to climb the next step and suddenly lost her balance when her sole came down on nothing but empty air. She stumbled forward and landed heavily on her hands and knees. She thought she might have cried out, but she had been so taken by surprise that she wasn't sure. Again panic welled up inside her, but again she fought it back down. *It's all right*, she told herself. *I've reached the top of the stairs, that's all. I'm on the first-floor landing now.*

She picked herself up and narrowed her watering eyes in order to pierce the misty gloom. Yes, she was on a landing piled high with an accumulation of old junk. Tendrils of smoke were already coming from what appeared to be wicker chair-legs as the fire heated the trapped air and the trapped air heated the wood.

Lauren edged around it and worked her way onto a narrow ribbon of landing, again obstructed by all manner of rubbish, old pieces of worn-out furniture or tin baths, empty bamboo birdcages . . .

She had fixed the position at which she had seen the little boy approximately in her mind, but to make absolutely sure she found the right flat, she resolved to stop at each front door in turn. The first had been left open, so sudden had been the departure of the occupants.

She took the handkerchief away from her mouth just long enough to call out, "Hello? Hello, is anyone there?"

She waited a moment. Nothing. She moved on to the next flat. This door was shut, so she had to bend down and call through the letter-box. Again she received no response.

That did not mean to say that the flat in question was empty, of course. Perhaps the occupant or occupants were already unconscious or worse. Then again, maybe the crackle and roar of the flames were drowning her voice.

Doggedly, however, she moved on to the next flat, knowing that she was rapidly running out of time. Bending, she opened the letter-box and peered through the narrow opening into the flat beyond. It looked exactly how she had imagined it to look; cramped, poorly-furnished, basic. It appeared to be deserted, but still she called out, "Hello! Is anyone in there? Can you hear me?"

Nothing.

From somewhere up above came a terrifying screech of rending metal and collapsing timbers. Again Lauren cried out and instinctively hunched herself against an expected landslide of girders and concrete slabs, but fortunately nothing happened. With effort she straightened back to her full height. The super-hot air was practically unbreathable now, and it was making her eyes stream. The tension and the adverse conditions were gradually sapping all the strength from her. But she dare not tarry here; the risk was too great.

She was just about to move on to the next flat when she thought she heard a high, shrill cry coming from somewhere inside the flat beside which she had just stopped. A sudden jolt of expectancy surged through her, pushing away some of her fatigue. She bent and opened the letter-box again, and this time, when she peered through the slit, she saw a little boy standing helplessly in the smoky passage and knew that she had been right all along — she *had* seen this round, smudged, tear-streaked, utterly hopeless face at the window just moments before!

The little boy was about eight years old. He looked quite tall for his age, though much of that was due to his thin, willowy build. He was dressed in a creased T-shirt, shorts and sandals. His hair was black, short and spiky. He appeared to be so confused by the fire that he was rooted to the spot.

"Here!" she called. "Over here, by the letter-box!"

His dark, scared eyes swivelled to lock upon her own, just visible through the pall of smoke. Relief, a slender reassurance that this woman might just be his salvation, made the tense hunch of his little shoulders drop and his lower lip tremble.

"Come on, we have to be quick!" Lauren called to him, licking her dry lips. "Are you all alone in there?"

He shook his head.

"Who else is with you?"

"Grandfather," said the little boy. Miserably he added, "He's sleeping."

That sounded ominous, Lauren thought, but she tried not to let it show. "What's your name?"

"Gordon Wong."

"All right, Gordon. Can you open the door? Do you know how to open the door?"

Even in his present predicament, the child was wary of her. Slowly, without once taking his eyes from that portion of her face that he could see through the letter-box, he nodded.

"Come and open it, then!" she called. "Quickly, now!"

He did not move at once. Then, slowly, he took one step forward. "That's it," she called to encourage him. "Hurry!" He came nearer, nearer. Outside and above, Lauren heard another rending crash of splintering wood and cracking concrete.

Smoke was rising from the passage floor now, growing so thick that Lauren could no longer see the little boy's feet as he came towards her. But he continued to approach the door, his large, liquid eyes fixed upon her, although his progress was hampered by a fear that had stiffened his joints and was slowing him down.

Lauren continued to coax him on, her voice authoritative but gentle. Whenever the child looked as if he might crack under the pressure, Lauren began to talk to him in Chinese, until at last he was at the door, where he reached up, pulled back the bolt —

Lauren wasted no time. As soon as the bolt was free she grasped the handle and opened the door. Trapped heat slapped her in the face and she rocked back a little with the force of it, but knew that as exhausted as she was, she still could not rest yet.

She scooped the tearful little boy up into her arms. Instinctively his own arms went around her neck and he clung to her.

"Where is your grandfather?" Lauren asked urgently.

He pointed back down the passage, to the living-room, where smoke was already growing as thick as pea-soup fog.

Now Lauren had to address yet another dilemma. Dare she go further into the flat to locate the boy's 'sleeping' grandparent, and thus endanger both her own life and that of the boy? It seemed like suicide. But what was the alternative? She could not leave another human being to die.

She had to make a snap decision, and so she did. "Don't worry," she said into the boy's left ear. "We'll go and fetch help." It was the best she could hope to do; to complete her rescue of the little boy and then find some firemen who had the experience and breathing apparatus needed to bring about a faster and more efficient rescue than anything she could hope to do.

Ignoring the little boy's desperate protests, she turned and retraced her steps back to the front door, out onto the landing, back past all the smouldering and smoking piles of discarded junk . . .

Smoke was everywhere. It made her eyes tingle and sting, crept inexorably and slyly through the handkerchief to infiltrate her mouth and nostrils. She clung to the little boy and he clung to her, both of them making scared little mewling sounds now, and she reached the head of the stairs with the roaring spit of flames threatening to deafen them both.

Carefully she put her foot down on the first step. Did it shift and creak a little beneath her weight, or was that just imagination? She took another step, another, one more. She could no longer see where she was going, for the smoke was thick enough to slice now, and her eyes were watering so badly that she could hardly keep them open.

She remembered what she had said to David the previous week, that she

162

enjoyed danger. But she had been wrong. This was danger, and she was not enjoying it one bit.

The little boy trembled in her grip. She held him still closer, muttering comforting nonsense to keep him from snapping altogether.

One more step . . . another . . .

Something else collapsed at the top of the building, and whatever it was sent a shockwave of oven-hot air down through the tenement, fanning the flames on the lower storeys and knocking Lauren forward so that she descended what remained of the staircase in a wild, disorderly rush.

At last her feet came down on level ground, and working on instinct now, for her senses had been so battered that she was staggering blindly, she turned and began to head for the vague, out-of-focus promise of dying daylight ahead.

What followed was confusion, and she would never really recall any of it to any great degree. She stumbled out into relatively fresh air, and the sudden cooling gust of it went some of the way to reviving her. Suddenly hands were upon her; the boy was taken from her grasp; she herself was steadied; urgent shouting replaced the greedy crackle of omnivorous flames; she was lowered down onto a stretcher; she heard someone calling her name, "Lauren! Lauren!" The voice was familiar; it was David. His voice cracked fearfully, and it came into her mind that she must look a mess, and that he thought he was about to lose her.

"Up . . . stairs . . . flat . . . seven . . . " She realised distantly and with a start that the strange, croaking voice was her own. "The boy's . . . grandfather . . . "

Another male voice said in Chinese, "Someone else up there? Quickly! You men — flat seven; an old man!"

Lauren allowed herself to relax a little then. No matter what happened now, she had done her best, rescued the little boy, and at least tried to put the rescue of his grandfather into action. All she could do now was pray, but before she could do that she drifted away on a tide of all-consuming unconsciousness . . . For a long, long time, there was nothing in Lauren's world except darkness and silence. Slowly light returned, a pinprick at first, which rapidly grew wider. When she was finally able to open her still-bloodshot eyes, it took her a moment to gather her bearings.

The clean smell of antiseptic and the vague, distant sounds of echoing footsteps and tannoy announcements told her that she was in a hospital bed. Craning her neck, she made a slow inspection of her surroundings. It looked as if they had put her in a private room, for she was all alone.

"Lauren! Thank God!"

She turned her head slowly towards the sound. David Kent was sitting on a chair by her bedside, his usually relaxed, handsome face now looking tight, strained and haggard beneath the room's harsh fluorescent lights.

"Da . . . vid . . . "

It hurt to talk; her voice was barely more than a whisper.

He reached out impulsively and covered her folded hands with his own. She thought for a moment that his eyes had taken on a liquid shine, but maybe it was just a trick of the light.

"Oh, Lauren, thank God, thank God . . . I thought you were going . . . " He bit back whatever he had been about to say, and gently set his weight down on the edge of the bed, his hands still covering hers. "How are you feeling?" he asked gently.

Lauren considered before replying. "Tired," she said at last, and indeed, she could feel her eyelids drooping even as she said it. "Sore . . . throat. Hard to . . . " She swallowed painfully. " . . . talk," she finished.

"I'll bet it is," he said, squeezing her hands. "Just rest. You're all right, now. Everything's been taken care of. Just get well."

"The fire — "

"Out," he replied. "They put it out yesterday evening." Her eyes grew wide and he confirmed what had just come into her mind. "Yes; you've been unconscious for the best part of a day."

As she digested that, he reached up to brush an errant lock of hair back from her forehead, and the gesture seemed so natural that she did not think to question it.

"What . . . " She cleared her throat. "What about Gordon Wong?"

"The boy you rescued?" he asked. "He's safe. They've put him just along the corridor, in the children's ward. He's tired and scared, as you'd expect, but there's no permanent damage."

"And . . . his . . . " Again she had to swallow.

"His grandfather?" David supplied, to save her the effort of speaking. "Thanks to you, the firemen got him out of that inferno just in time. He's in intensive care right now. But the doctors seem hopeful that he'll pull through."

"David . . . ?"

"Yes?"

"I'm . . . I'm sorry for what I said to you . . . about your . . . being jealous, I mean . . . "

Again he squeezed her hand. "Don't worry about it. If it's any consolation, I'm sorry, too. I had no right to pry into your private life. I was just being over-protective, I suppose. Now just rest. I'll be here if you need me."

She closed her eyes. Now that she knew that everything was well, she could allow herself to relax again. But just before she drifted off to sleep, she was sure she felt David's cool, soft lips brush gently against her forehead, and she was certain that it was not just her imagination.

★ ★ ★

When Lauren awoke the following morning, she felt much better, though her eyes remained light-sensitive and her throat continued to feel sore.

Never one to remain inactive for long, however, she soon persuaded one of the nurses to allow her to get up, and clad in a dressing-gown and slippers that Maggie had brought from the flat for her, she shuffled along to the nearest pay-phone.

She wanted to call Ricky Lee and apologise for not keeping their date on Wednesday night. She knew he would understand; he had doubtless heard about the harbour-front fire, and quite possibly someone had told him of her own involvement in it. Still, she felt she owed him a personal explanation. He had been so kind to her that it was the least she could do.

She got the number of Silver Crop Studios from a helpful operator and dialled. When the voice at the other end of the line asked her who she wished to speak to, she gave the name of Ricky's secretary, Angela Yuen. A moment later, Angela's voice came into her ear. "Yes? May I help you?"

"Oh, yes. Hello. It's Lauren Adams here."

There was a pause. "Lauren Adams?" Angela Yuen asked uncertainly.

Lauren was a bit surprised that the secretary had forgotten her name so quickly. "Yes. From *The Ex-Pat*. I interviewed Ricky last Tuesday."

"Ah, yes. I'm sorry. How may I help you, Miss Adams?"

"Well, I don't suppose Ricky's there, is he?"

"I'm afraid not."

"I just wanted a quick word with him. You see, I had to break a date with him a couple of nights ago and I wanted to explain why." Angela Yuen said nothing, so Lauren suggested, "Perhaps it would be easier if you could get him to give me a call."

"Certainly. What is your number?"

Lauren gave out her telephone number at the flat, thanked the secretary and then rang off.

Her next job was to get directions to the children's ward, where she intended to visit young Gordon Wong.

At first glance, the ward was in chaos. Sunshine filled the large, airy room, as did the cheerful hubbub of chattering and playing children. In one corner sat a stack of old, colourful toys, around which several of the healthier children sat or sprawled, deep in play. Lauren saw that the less fortunate patients, who had to remain in bed, simply slept or read books and comics. When she asked the ward sister where she would find Gordon Wong, a troubled look came into the woman's face.

She pointed. "He is in the last bed on the left."

"*M goi.*"

Lauren felt a chill of apprehension, for the nurse's expression had unsettled her. Following the nurse's directions, however, she soon came to the little Oriental boy's bed.

Gordon's hands were clasped peacefully atop his white cotton sheet, and he was staring up at the ceiling through wide, dark eyes. She saw at once that he looked thoroughly miserable, and knowing how hospitals could affect some children, she promptly resolved to cheer him up.

Forcing a smile onto her sore, heat-flushed face, she came to a halt at his bedside. "Good morning, Gordon," she said as brightly as her raw throat would allow. "Do you remember me?"

He made no attempt to take his eyes away from some faraway spot beyond the ward ceiling, and gave no indication at all that he was even aware of her presence.

"Gordon?" she prompted.

At last his big hazel eyes came around to focus on her face, but there was no light of greeting in them, and no flicker of a smile on the narrow line of his mouth.

"Do you remember me, Gordon?" she tried again, resting her weight gently on the edge of his mattress.

He nodded, but that was all.

Disconcerted, she frowned. "Are you all right?" she asked, trying to make her hoarse voice reflect her genuine concern and willingness to help. "Don't you feel very well?"

He made no response.

"Are you worried about your grandfather?" she asked. "If you are, there's no need. The doctors say he will be fine, given time." She paused. "Gordon?"

Stubbornly, the little boy refused to break his silence. He merely turned his attention back to the ceiling, dismissing her with the gesture, and as she stood up to go, she saw a single, salty tear fill his right eye and slide erratically down his smooth cheek.

Mystified, and determined to find out what was troubling him, she went to see if the ward sister would prove to be any more communicative.

★ ★ ★

Lauren's doctors were pleased with her progress, and discharged her the following day. Pleased to be leaving hospital, she rang Maggie and made arrangements for her flat-mate to pick her up. As glad as she was to be going home, however, she could not shake off the troubled feeling that preoccupied her.

"Were there any calls for me while I was away?" she asked as Maggie drove them out of the hospital carpark and onto the expressway.

The Chinese girl thought a moment before shaking her head. "No. Were you expecting to hear from anyone special?"

Lauren kept her eyes on the road ahead. "No." But she was a little disappointed that Ricky had not returned her call.

She had lost all track of time. Somehow the week had flown past and they had reached the weekend again — the weekend Lauren had agreed to share with Maggie at Maggie's parents' place in Tsim Sha Tsui. The young Chinese girl understood completely when Lauren suggested they cancel the arrangement, and was all for stopping behind herself to help nurse Lauren back to full health, but Lauren insisted that she go on as planned. "I'm sure you'd rather spend some time with your fiance than looking after an old convalescent like me," she teased good-humouredly.

Maggie was reluctant to leave her, but eventually Lauren convinced her that she would be all right on her own. About an hour after they reached the flat, she was waving the Chinese girl off with a tired smile.

Now it was restful to have the flat to herself, to do however she felt with no-one but herself to consider. She spent the day reading, sleeping, watching TV and generally doing whatever she could to help her body heal itself completely. By the end of the day, she was certainly beginning to feel like her old self, though still she was troubled by the conversation she'd had with the ward sister about Gordon Wong.

At six o'clock that evening, just as she was drying herself off from a most envigorating shower, the telephone rang. Brushing her damp hair back from her face, she picked up the phone. "Hello?"

"Lauren, it's David."

The sound of his strong, low voice in her ear raised her spirits still further, and a smile spread slowly across her face without her realising it. "David. Well, as you can hear, I'm home."

"Yes. I just rang the hospital and they said you'd been discharged. I'm only sorry I wasn't there to meet you."

"Don't worry about it."

"How are you feeling, anyway?"

"Better."

He paused a moment before saying, "You gave me one heck of a fright, you know. When you came staggering out of that burning tenement . . . But so long as you're on the mend now."

"I am."

"Lauren . . . "

"Yes?"

"Have you got anything planned for tomorrow?"

"No."

"Then I wonder if you'd let me take you to lunch?"

She wasn't sure about that. Oh, the prospect of spending time with David, just the two of them, away from their working environment, certainly appealed, but there were other considerations. She had suffered no really bad injuries, it was true, but it would be some time before the small, irritating red marks on her face cleared up completely. "I don't know . . . "

"If you're not up to it," he said understandingly, his voice so gentle and relaxing that she found just the tone of it somehow soothing, "don't worry. But I . . . well, I just wanted to do something to tell you what your recovery means to me . . . "

"There's no need for that," she insisted.

"Oh, yes there is," he replied simply.

Something occurred to Lauren then. "All right, David. Thank you very much," she said. "There's something

I'd like to talk to *you* about, actually."

"That sounds ominous."

"It isn't," she replied. "At least, I don't think so."

"All right," he said. "Pick you up at two?"

"I'll be waiting."

There was another pause, almost as if he were trying to decide how best to close such an unusually informal conversation with her. At last he said, "God bless, then. Sleep well," and it was such a simple and yet charming thing to say that the emotions she had for him swelled suddenly until she did not think her heart could possibly contain all the love she felt for him.

Love?

The hand holding the receiver paused mid-way through the act of hanging up, for the word, her first true understanding of her feelings for him, came as something of a shock.

Her natural instinct was to dismiss the notion. She had never been a romantic before coming here to this island of far eastern promise. Why should she start now? It was just the exotic atmosphere of the place, the sudden, dramatic turn her life had taken . . .

Wasn't it?

Slowly she set the receiver down on its cradle. If she was going to be totally honest with herself — and she had never been anything else in her entire life — she didn't know. She really *didn't* know.

* * *

Sunday morning dawned bright and cheerful, and Lauren felt better than she had in days. Although she made a determined effort to keep everything in perspective, however, and not allow her heart to rule her head, she could hardly wait for the morning to pass and two o'clock to arrive.

At a quarter to two, the front-door bell gave a buzz she was eager to answer.

David was standing in the hallway with a broad grin on his face and a large bunch of flowers in one hand. "For you," he said.

She took the flowers with a pleasant tingle of surprise, her smile every bit as broad as his own, and invited him inside.

"I've booked a table for two-thirty," he said. "I hope that's not too early for you."

"No, that's fine."

They faced each other in the narrow passage, each acutely aware of the nearness of the other.

"Well," he said, looking down at her. "You're certainly looking better."

"I feel it."

He watched her take the flowers through to the kitchen and search the cupboards for a vase. He looked tanned and fit in grey trousers and white polo shirt, his old athletic self now that she too had started to resemble the girl she had been before the fire in the tenement.

"Can I get you a drink or something?" she asked over her shoulder.

"No, better not. It's quite a drive from here to the restaurant, so we'd better get moving in a while."

"Where are we going?"

"There's a nice Szechuan restaurant up in Happy Valley," he said. "I think you'll like it."

Before she could stop herself she said, "Not the Red Pond?"

He appeared surprised. "You know it?"

She avoided his gaze, because it was the very same restaurant that Ricky had taken her to the previous week. "I've . . . heard of it." She felt the lie was justified, to save him from any hurt he might feel knowing that another man had taken her there first.

They left the flat shortly afterwards and travelled downstairs to where David had parked his car. It felt good to be on something like friendly terms with him again, as if a weight had been lifted. No, not just good. *Marvellous.*

8

They drove through the city and on towards Happy Valley, where they joined up with traffic heading towards the race-meetings which were held there every Sunday.

The restaurant was as plush and expensive as she remembered it, but although she was sure his salary as a newspaper editor in no way compared to that of a superstar like Ricky Lee's, money was no object as far as David was concerned. He was so grateful that she had escaped serious injury, he appeared to want the entire world to know it.

"I know we've had our ups and downs these past few weeks," he said after they'd ordered and were waiting for their *hors d'ouvres* to arrive. "But . . . well, seeing the way you looked at the hospital . . . Lauren . . . " Reaching for his wine glass, he searched for the right words. "I suppose what I'm trying to say is, well; life can be so fragile, it made me realise that the time we spend here on earth is precious . . . so precious that we shouldn't waste a moment of it. Does that sound a bit corny, do you think?"

She smiled gently. "I think it sounds rather philosophical," she replied. "And very sensible."

"You remember that evening at your flat, when . . . "

She remembered, all right, and to save him further embarrassment, she said, "Yes, I remember."

"Well," he said. "I think you know the reason I kissed you. I was attracted to you from the first moment I saw you, but I just didn't realise it at the time. There was something about you, some inner quality that drew me to you. And, well, tell me if I'm wrong, but . . . I flatter myself to think that you felt it too, that special something between us?"

"I did," she confessed softly.

"So I lost my head," he said as he released a sigh. "That night, coming to see you the way I did, I just couldn't help myself. I *had* to kiss you."

"But then you had second thoughts," she said. This was becoming embarrassing, but she thought it better to have the thing out once and for all, in order to really be able to start afresh.

"Yes," he admitted. "Well, no, not really. What I started thinking about was my position as your employer . . . I mean, it was all happening so fast . . . I didn't want you to think that I was trying to take advantage of you, so I decided to back off, give you some space. If anything was going to happen between us, it would be best if it moved at its own pace."

Fighting to keep her voice even, she said, "David — what exactly are you trying to say?"

He hesitated for just a moment before taking the plunge. "That I'm in l — "

He broke off suddenly and a look of alarm entered his eyes as he focused on something over her shoulder. She frowned at him worriedly. "David? Are you all right?"

He looked clearly ill at ease now. "Uh, yes, yes, sure."

But he was a terrible liar, and before he could stop her, she turned around in order to see what had alarmed him so.

At once she understood.

Ricky Lee had just arrived at the restaurant and was being shown to a table on the far side of the dining area by a most attentive waiter. Taken alone, of course, there was nothing remarkable in that. Lauren herself had been here with Ricky five days before. But now, as she saw the film star striding towards his table with one attractive, dark-haired Oriental girl on each arm, all three of them punctuating their conversation with the odd kiss and rather shameless fondle, she realised that David had been hoping she would not notice them, and thus spare herself some hurt and disappointment.

She turned back to face David, just as the girls giggled high and unrestrained at some witticism Ricky had muttered. She drew in a deep breath, aware that David was watching her closely, sober-faced.

"So," she said at last, as their starters came. "It seems as if you were right, David. Ricky *does* seem to have something of a reputation."

He waited until their waiter had gone before saying sincerely, "I'm only sorry you had to find out this way. I'd never have brought you here if I'd thought — "

"No matter," she said quietly.

He paused a moment, eyeing her carefully. "Did he mean anything to you?" he asked cautiously.

Much to his relief, she smiled. "I only knew him for a day," she replied simply. "Oh, he was very charming. But I owe you an apology. I realise now that you were only trying to warn me before I became just one more name on his list of victims."

"Try not to feel too bad about it," David counselled. "You're not the first woman he's ever taken in, and sad to say, I don't suppose you'll be the last."

She forced the film star from her mind, although she felt very sad that he had failed to live up to the personable image he presented to the world.

"Anyway," said David. "What was it you wanted to speak to me about?"

"I'm sorry?"

"On the phone yesterday evening," he reminded her. "You said there was something you wanted to speak to me about."

"Oh, yes."

He glanced across at her. "Are you sure it's nothing ominous?"

"Well . . . yes and no, really," she replied awkwardly. "It's just that . . . well, I know I've only been with *The Ex-Pat* for a few weeks, David, but — I'd like to take a leave of absence, if I may."

He frowned. "Leave of absence?"

"Yes. Just a week, if that."

He thought he understood. "You'd like to go home for a while. Well, I can't say that I blame you there. One way or another, you haven't had many dull moments since you set foot in Hong Kong."

"No, it's not to go home, David," she said.

"Oh?"

She toyed with her food. "You remember Gordon Wong, the little boy from the tenement?"

"Yes."

"Well, I visited him while I was in hospital; you know, just to see how he was getting on." Her eyes came up to meet his. "He's desperately unhappy, David. According to the ward sister I spoke to, he was sent to live with his grandfather about two years ago, after his parents were killed in a monsoon.

"Well, his grandfather looks as if he'll be spending quite some time in hospital over the next couple of months. All the smoke he inhaled has activated some sort of respiratory problem in him. Even when he's allowed to go back to what's left of his home, it's doubtful that he'll be able to look after Gordon."

David eyed her over the rim of his wine glass. "What's the alternative, then?"

"For the boy?" Lauren shook her head. "They're talking about sending him to an orphanage."

David frowned. "That's crazy. The orphanages on this island are practically full to bursting as it is."

"I know. But there is another alternative. Gordon was born and brought up just outside Wuzhou, in Guangxi Province. His father's brother still runs a farm there."

"And you think someone should take the boy to live with his uncle."

"Yes."

"You," he said.

She nodded.

"Lauren," he said sincerely, "I appreciate your motives. I'm not in the least bit surprised that you want to help the poor tike."

"I feel . . . well, responsible for him, in a way," she said.

"That's understandable. But do you know what you're suggesting? In the first place, you'll need to get permission from the Chinese government before you can return the boy to the mainland — "

"That should be no problem. He's a Chinese subject, anyway."

"All right. But do you have any idea of the geography involved? Where Wuzhou is, exactly?"

"Well, no."

"Then let me tell you. It's about three hundred kilometres east of here, possibly a little more — yes, a bit more than you'd bargained for, I can tell by the expression on your face." Putting his glass down, he moderated his tone. "Look, don't get me wrong. Your heart's in the right place. But I'm just trying to be practical. Where are you going to get the money to finance this little expedition of yours?

And who's to say that the boy *wants* to go and live with his uncle, much less whether his uncle wants to take him in?" As much as Lauren hated to admit it, his words made her realise that she hadn't really considered all the angles of her proposition yet. But she refused to abandon it. She had seen the sorrow etched into Gordon's young face. No child should have to suffer so wretchedly. And as she had already said, she felt responsible for the boy.

"I've already made some enquiries," she said. "I spoke briefly with Gordon's grandfather. He believes that his son — Gordon's uncle — would be only too pleased to take the boy now. A few years ago, when Gordon's parents died, the farm he runs was barely self-supporting. That's why the boy was sent to live with the old man, here in Hong Kong. Now, though, that's all changed. The farm has flourished. As much as anything else, Gordon's uncle would probably value his help around the place, and it would certainly be an ideal environment for Gordon to grow up in."

"Perhaps you ought to write and confirm that with the uncle himself before you take the matter any further."

"I already have. I sent him a letter explaining everything that's happened, and I expect a reply any day now."

"And what about the boy? Does he want to go back to live in China?"

"What's the alternative?" she asked. "He's already spent two years living in an overcrowded tenement. Now it looks as if he'll spend several more living in an overcrowded orphanage — unless somebody does something about it."

David was silent for a moment.

"Well?" she said. "What do you think?"

"Do you want my honest opinion, Lauren?"

"Of course."

"I don't like it. I don't like it one little bit. You'd be a woman travelling alone. Anything could happen to you between here and there." He shook his head. "My advice is this; suggest your idea to the authorities. Let them handle it."

The smile that played briefly across Lauren's full lips was cynical, and David knew why. Even with the best will in the world, the system of government in any country is geared up to accommodate the wishes of the masses, not the individual.

"I'm sorry that you don't feel my idea has merit,"she said without rancour. "Nevertheless, I'd appreciate it if you would allow me to take a weeks' leave sometime in the not-too-distant future."

He clearly wasn't happy about it. "You're really intent on going through with it?"

"Yes. Somehow I'm going to take Gordon Wong back to the province in which he was born, and reunite him with his uncle and the rest of his family. And if you can't see your way clear to allowing me to take some leave to accomplish it — unpaid leave, if necessary — then I'll have to resign, David. As much as I'd hate to do it, I'll resign."

It was ironic that just as their relationship seemed to be blossoming at last, Lauren's insistence on taking the young Oriental boy back to Guangxi Province had set up some sort of invisible barrier between them again. But Lauren was nothing if not stubborn, and once her mind was made up, nothing on earth could change it.

She received a letter from Gordon's uncle, Carter Wong, about three days later. As Gordon's grandfather had said, the Wong farm had indeed flourished, and Carter Wong said he would be delighted to take charge of his brother's only son. In her lunch-break, Lauren travelled back to the hospital, where the authorities had decided to keep young Gordon while they found a place for him at one of the child-care centres dotted throughout the city, and showed the boy his uncle's letter.

"Would you like to go back to Guangxi Province, Gordon?" she asked him softly.

For the first time, she saw some animation on his face that was not motivated by either fear or sorrow. His dark eyes moved up from the letter to her face. "Could my grandfather come, too?" he asked in a low, shy voice.

"Not right away," she explained. "He's still very ill. But maybe in a few months."

The boy thought it over, though there was really very little to consider. "I would like to go," he told her.

"Then you shall," she said.

As she left the hospital, however, Lauren felt that her problems were only just beginning. She had set herself a difficult task. As David had pointed out, she had no way to finance the journey. It looked as if she would have to leave her job in order to see the thing through. And what made it worse was the fact that there could be no backing

195

out now. She had promised the child. She simply could not let him down.

When she got back to the office, she sat down at her desk and tried to concentrate on her work, but it was no good; her mind was still on the task she had set herself.

Impulsively she got up and went across to David's office, where she knocked on the door and said softly, "Could I have a word?"

He looked up from behind his desk and smiled at her. "Sure. Come in."

"I'm not disturbing you, am I?"

"Of course not. What can I do for you?"

"It's about Gordon Wong."

The smile left his lips. "Ah."

"I heard from his uncle today, confirming what we already assumed; that if I can get the boy to him, he'd be happy to have him live there."

"You've told the boy?" David asked.

"Yes. At lunch-time."

"And he's happy about it, too?"

"Very much so."

"Then you want to take some leave," he guessed.

"Well . . . not right away. I still have to find the money for the trip yet, but . . . "

He tossed his pen down onto a pile of copy he'd been editing. "The money's no problem," he said softly.

She looked at him curiously. "I'm sorry?"

"You've got one week in which to make the trip," he told her tonelessly, "and enough money to cover all the expenses you're likely to incur — courtesy of *The Ex-Pat*."

She could hardly believe her ears. "But — "

"On one condition," he cut in. "That you write the entire experience up into something we can serialise over three or four issues. That's how I've talked the board of directors into financing the trip, by promising them a series of heartwarming features that will boost our circulation."

She was dumbfounded. "David . . . of

197

course. I mean . . . that's fantastic!"
Again she felt a sudden, giddying
burst of affection for this selfless,
understanding man. "Thank you, David.
I know you don't approve of what I'm
going to do, but that only makes me
appreciate what you've done for me all
the more."

"Just promise me you'll come back
safely," he said, standing up and
coming around the desk to place
his palms lightly on her shoulders
and squeeze them tenderly. "That's
all I ask."

"I promise," she said. "I promise I'll
come back to you."

★ ★ ★

The next few days passed in a
riot of activity, as Lauren set about
obtaining the necessary permissions
and permits she would need before
she could embark upon her three
hundred kilometre trek to Wuzhou.
She learned something of British and

Chinese red tape in that time, but with patience — a quality she had learned from David — and her usual iron determination, she slowly overcame one bureaucratic hurdle after another.

Somehow everything managed to sort itself out, though, and within a week, Lauren was appointed as Gordon Wong's temporary guardian for the duration of the journey from Hong Kong to the Wong family farm in Guangxi Province.

David was a great help during that time, and a tower of strength, particularly when it came to helping plot the route she and Gordon Wong would take to reach the boy's uncle's farm on the outskirts of the Chinese city. With maps spread across the desk and guidebooks piled up on the visitor's chair, they worked late into the evening deciding upon the best route she should travel.

At last David straightened up and stretched his spine, then turned to look down at her. "Well," he said with a wry smile. "I hope you're a good sailor, Lauren, because it looks as if you'll be making most of the journey by boat."

Refolding the maps and putting them in her bag, she said quietly, "Thank you, David. You've helped me more than you know. I couldn't have done any of this without you."

He shrugged. "We wouldn't be doing any of it at all if it weren't for your bravery in rescuing Gordon in the first place." He glanced at his wristwatch. "It's been a long day. What say we find a restaurant and have something to eat before I run you home?"

"Well, I'm not really that hungry . . . "

He smiled. "Nerves settling in at last?"

She smiled back, ruefully. "Yes, I think they are, now that all of this is finally becoming a reality."

He reached for his jacket. "All right. A sandwich, then?"

"Yes, that would be nice."

They left the office behind them,

collected his car from the small car-park at the end of the block and then drove to a sandwich bar, where they took their food away. He drove them out of the city then, up into the forested slopes that rose so majestically above the metropolis below, and with probably one of the best views in the world before them, they unwrapped their sandwiches and eased the lids off their polystyrene cups of coffee and just sat there, side by side, in the gathering dusk.

It was an evening she would remember for a long time to come, for the easy companionship they shared and for the sheer pleasure of his calming presence.

At last he drove her back to the flat and saw her to her front door, where he waited until she had fumbled her key from her purse. "You'll be all right, now?" he asked.

"Yes, thanks."

"Well . . . goodnight, then . . . "

He was just turning away when she called his name, impulsively.

He turned back to face her. "Yes?"

Acting purely on instinct now, knowing intuitively that it was the right thing to do, she reached up and kissed him gently on the cheek, enjoying the warmth coming off his skin, the subtle herbs-and-spices smell of him.

He looked down at her, vaguely surprised by her gesture, but pleasantly so, then reached down and ran a hand through her hair in a gentle caress.

"You know how I feel about you, don't you?" he said softly.

She avoided his gaze, knowing that the last vestiges of her ability to resist him would crumble if she gazed directly into his dark, depthless eyes. "I know how you *think* you feel."

She sensed his frown. "What does that mean?" he asked, puzzled.

She shrugged, somehow tongue-tied and unable to express herself as coherently as she would have liked. "I know how *I* feel about you, David. But . . . is it for real, or is it just the magic of this island that makes us feel the way we do?"

He shook his head in disbelief. "You think it's the 'magic of the island' that's influencing the way I feel about you?"

"Can you honestly say that it isn't?" she countered.

"Yes. But you . . . "

Again she shrugged. "I'm not sure, David. That's the trouble . . . I'm just not sure."

He nodded slowly. "Well, when you *are* sure, you know where to find me," he said, his tone as soft and gentle and understanding as ever. "I'll be waiting for you."

"I know," she said. "I'm sorry, David — "

"Don't be," he interrupted. "I know how I feel about you, Lauren. I think I fell in love with you just a little bit the first time we met, at your interview in London, so I know for a fact that it's certainly nothing to do with Hong Kong — and I'll prove it to you, in time."

He reached down and kissed her gently on the forehead, then stood back and waited until she had let herself into the flat before turning and walking away.

At last the morning of Lauren's departure to Guangxi Province arrived, and since the ferry she had elected to take from Kowloon to Canton left at nine o'clock, she had to get an early start. It was just after dawn when she carried her luggage — just enough clothes and toiletries for the week, all packed into a smart zip-up carrier with a shoulder-strap — down to the car with butterflies in her tummy. When she came back up to tell Maggie that she was ready to go, the Oriental girl was in the living-room, just putting the phone down.

"Oh, what a shame," she said.

"I'm sorry?"

"Mr David just called," Maggie explained. "He says he is sorry, but that he will not be able to come to the wharf to see you off. There has been a problem at the office and he has to deal with it."

The news came as quite a blow. The prospect of not seeing David for one entire week had been bad enough, but the fact that he would not even be there to see her off left her feeling badly disappointed. Still, there was no help for it, and in any case, the coming week should fly past, hopefully. Putting on a brave face, she said, "No matter. I'm . . . ah . . . all ready to go when you are." Maggie was. They went back downstairs to the car and Maggie drove them through the still, grey city with the sun rising sluggishly in the east. They parked at the hospital, where Lauren went inside and, after showing the necessary papers, collected Gordon Wong. The boy was understandably eager to leave hospital, though he insisted on saying goodbye to his grandfather first. After that, they both climbed into Maggie's car and drove through the Cross-Harbour Tunnel into Kowloon. At the Tai Kok

Tsui Wharf, the Chinese girl waved them up the gangplank and onto the Pearl River Shipping Company vessel *Tianhu*.

The large, spotless ferry sailed promptly at nine, ploughing regally away from the wharf and into the choppy blue-green waters of the South China Sea. Lauren and Gordon stood by the rail watching the concrete sprawl of Kowloon grow small in the distance. A cooling, salty sea-breeze brought some relief from the near-constant humidity, and the steady throbbing of the *Tianhu*'s engines was broken by the cries of wheeling gulls above.

Standing there, Lauren thought about the journey ahead. Was David right? Did it really hold the possibility of danger? Surely not. But, as he had pointed out, she was a woman travelling alone. She did not want to allow doubt to slip into her mind, but it was insistent and intrusive, and she could not shut it out.

But then something happened to

banish it from her mind. Entirely without warning, Gordon Wong reached up and took hold of her hand, and when she glanced down at him and he smiled back up at her with shy gratitude plain in his eyes, she realised that she was not just a woman travelling alone. She had a responsibility, in the shape of this little boy, and that knowledge filled her with a determination to succeed come what may.

9

The day passed slowly, but the ferry continued to plough north until the South China Sea finally gave way to the Pearl River. Dusk smudged the sky, turning slowly to evening, and eventually reflected moonlight danced and skittered across the rippling water that surrounded them.

Lauren knew that to have made the journey by hovercraft would have been quicker and more direct, but it would also have been more expensive, and in any case, this more leisurely journey would hopefully give her more time in which to get to know her young ward, and provide more background information for her projected series of features on the experience.

Gordon surprised her by being enormously intelligent, though somewhat shy. Not only was he good at mathematics and science, he also enjoyed art and writing, and once he overcame his basic wariness, he regaled her with an endless flow of stories he'd made up, and odd, interesting facts he'd picked up at school. He was not a very good traveller, however, and after a while the constant motion of the ferry made him feel a little nauseous.

The *Tianhu* arrived at Zhoutouzui Wharf in Canton at seven o'clock the following morning, and when they disembarked they found the city to be every bit as busy as Hong Kong. All the chaos was just a little bit frightening as well, though, so they found a relatively quiet place in which to eat and study their guidebooks, and then went in search of the boat that would take them further north, up the Pearl, and then Xi, Rivers. By late afternoon, they were on their way again, ploughing steadily deeper into China.

It was a vast, wild country, she saw now, and it seemed to stretch away from either bank in a con fused and endless tangle of greenery. One northward mile followed another, though, and at last the boat docked at Wuzhou.

By the time they reached the city, however, it was too late to complete their journey to the Wong farm, even if the buses had still been running, so Lauren found them a hotel at which to spend the night. Here she was able to enjoy a refreshing bath and sleep in a soft bed that did not rock biliously to and fro beneath her. Even Gordon's spirits picked up now that he knew the last of the water-travel was behind them.

Early the next morning they went in search of the bus that would take them on the last leg of their journey to the Wong farm. Not so very long afterwards, they climbed aboard a crowded — and frankly rather old — bus and rattled out into the countryside, leaving Wuzhou behind them.

Conditions aboard the bus were

crude, to say the least. It appeared that the vehicle had little in the way of suspension and that the driver had yet to pass any type of formal driving test. Neither did the rutted goat-track that passed for a road help much. As the morning wore on the bus grew hotter and more stuffy, and at every stop more and more people got on, though few got off.

At about mid-day the bus began to make a strange clunking sound, and leaning forward in her seat, Lauren saw steam escaping from beneath the bonnet. At last the driver pulled over to the side of the road and made a brief, perfunctory apology for the delay. Obviously much used to the vagaries of his vehicle, he promptly pulled a tool-kit from beneath his seat and suggested that his passengers take the opportunity to alight and stretch their legs until he could persuade the temperamental engine to re-start. Since Gordon had been showing signs of travel-sickness again, Lauren needed no second urging.

They climbed down onto a dirt road fringed by thick-boled trees, where heat bouncing up off the potholed track struck them with all the force of a slap, threatening to dehydrate them very quickly. Mosquitoes buzzed and sliced the thick air around them.

To give the little boy something to take his mind off his queasiness, Lauren said, "Let's go exploring, shall we?"

Relieved to be out in the open air after spending so long in the confines of the bus, he too was anxious to stretch his legs. "Yes."

Hand in hand, they left the rest of the passengers behind them and strolled into the forest. Lauren had expected it to be a little cooler within its gloomy confines, but if anything it was hotter, because the interlaced branches overhead trapped the air. Gordon seemed happy enough to race off ahead though, determined to take all of these new sights and sounds in at once, and she watched him with a fond smile playing across her tired face.

She came to a deadfall and sat down, setting her luggage beside her. The bus journey had taken more out of them both than she had realised. She watched Gordon examine trees, vines and lianas, then search the loamy soil for animal tracks. Here and there bars of dusty sunlight filtered down through the foliage above, giving the glade a weird, surreal look. But as hot and gloomy as it was, it was peaceful too, after the cough and growl of the bus's engine and the more general hubbub of the many passengers.

It was so peaceful, in fact, that when the bus roared to life some indeterminate time later, the sound of it made Lauren start. As she sprang to her feet, she realised that the torpid air had lulled her into a doze, and that consequently she had lost all track of time. But now that the driver had managed to get his bus working again, they had better get back to it.

"Gordon!" she called. "Come on! Time we were getting back!"

The little boy was a few hundred feet away, playing with a fallen branch he had found. Hearing her voice, he tossed the stick away and raced back to her, waving as he came. By the time he reached her, Lauren had hoisted her luggage back over her shoulder, and taking the boy's hand, she led them back through the forest, heading for the bright, nearly white sunlight beyond the last of the distant trees, where the road dribbled on towards the east. Again they heard the engine of the bus growl as the driver pressed the accelerator — but this time the sound filled Lauren with a sense of unease.

She frowned. It sounded as if the driver of the bus were moving off. But surely she was mistaken? He wouldn't just drive off without them, would he? Lauren knew with a sinking feeling that he might, if he was anxious enough to make up the time they'd already lost, and if he genuinely believed that all of his passengers had climbed back on board.

Abruptly she broke into a run. "Quickly, Gordon! Hurry, now!"

They dodged all the trees in their path and kicked up little divots of dead leaves and loamy soil, but by the time they burst back out onto the road, the bus was already several hundred yards distant, and widening the gap with every moment.

Frantically they both waved to attract attention, but great clouds of exhaust obscured whatever view the driver might have had of the track behind him.

The bus grew smaller and smaller until even the erratic rumble of its engine could no longer be heard. Dispiritedly, Lauren set her bag down and turned around to examine their surroundings. It looked as if they had inadvertently stranded themselves in the middle of nowhere.

She looked back the way they had

come. How far back had the last stop been? She really hadn't been paying too much attention, but something told her that it had been quite a way. Next she looked up the road in the direction the bus had just gone. Was there a stop anywhere near to hand ahead? Again, she had no way of knowing for certain. But one thing was definite. This road was little used. There was practically no chance of flagging down a passing motorist and hitching a ride. The only option left to them was to walk until they came to something approaching civilisation — or until another infrequent bus came along.

In such heat, even the slightest effort quickly drained away energy, and although they started off at a good and determined pace, it wasn't long before each step grew slower and the effort of just walking grew harder. To make matters worse, dark storm-clouds began to gather up ahead, threatening a monsoon.

After two hours and possibly four or five miles, they came to a fork in the road. Lauren searched in vain for a signpost, but evidently such things did not extend to this remote part of the hinterland.

Which way should they go, then?

It was going to be a tricky decision. On the one hand, they might be close to their destination now. But if she elected to take the wrong turning, she might lead them miles out of their way.

Glancing down at Gordon, she saw how weary he was. Like it or not, then, she would have to call a halt.

They found a deadfall by the road and sat down, and Lauren rummaged in her bag for the selection of sweets she had purchased in Wuzhou for the journey. By this time they were both hungry, and the sweets weren't nearly enough to satisfy them, but there was little option. With her face now smudged by travel and looking as unglamorous as it was possible to look, Lauren told herself not to give up hope. Sooner or later they *must* come to civilisation, even if it was just another stop-over for the bus route.

The pounding heat made them feel drowsy, though finally, when Lauren judged that they'd rested long enough, they climbed back to their feet and stood facing the fork in the road.

"Do you remember this region at all, Gordon?" she asked, knowing that it was a long-shot.

Gordon shook his head.

"All right," Lauren muttered, half to herself. She studied their choices, hoping for instinct to point them in the right direction. There was little to choose between the two roads, however. Each was little more than a rutted, hard-packed dirt track bordered by wild tangles of undergrowth and shadow-filled forest. "We'll take the left fork," she decided at length.

They continued walking.

They trudged on as the afternoon waned around them and the storm-clouds continued to gather. Time and again Lauren glanced over her shoulder, hoping to find a car or van coming towards them, but the road remained stubbornly empty.

At last, with evening approaching, the first large drops of rain began to fall, tapping at the dusty ground with soft, liquidy fingers. The sky had taken on the colour of an angry bruise now, as the rain began to come down heavier, already forming puddles in the ruts and pot-holes.

For Lauren, it was almost the last straw. How could events have conspired to put them in this predicament? It all seemed so unfair. But standing here bemoaning her fate would accomplish nothing.

"Come on," she said, having to raise her voice to be heard. "We'd best shelter under the trees."

The storm broke with full force just as they entered the dark, shadowy forest. The southwesterly wind picked up in a series of buffeting gusts, the rain fell harder and in the distance, thunder rumbled like cannon-fire.

Gordon clung to her so hard that she felt his nails digging into her palm, but she was as unnerved by the fury of the cloud-burst as he was. Eventually she scooped him up into her arms and went deeper into the forest in search of shelter.

Rain fell diagonally in a shifting wall of water, needling the puddles with billions of tiny pin-pricks. At least the branches overhead kept most of it off, though; that was something. Still . . . Lauren paused a moment to look up. The branches were whipping back and forth with a harsh rattle and rustle of leaves as the storm-force wind rocked them this way and that. Beyond them, she saw purple clouds racing across the leaden sky.

Thunder rumbled and crashed. Lightning struck the earth with a sharp, accusing finger. She had to caution herself against panic, although it was hard to believe that this was *not* the end of the world.

Distracted by so much chaos, Lauren tripped on an exposed tree-root and stumbled forward. It was only by luck that she managed to keep her balance. Terrified, Gordon clung to her with fingers turned to talons. She found herself muttering into his ear, "It's all right, it's all right, it's only a storm . . . "

At last she found a spot where the tightly-packed trees would offer them some semblance of protection, and set the boy down. They could hardly see each other by this time, because it was so dark, and each was just a silhouette to the other. That could have been why the boy remained so close to her, because he was afraid that the shadows would creep up on them both and snatch her away from him.

They familiarised themselves with their new surroundings mostly by touch. Eventually Lauren sat down on a little tussock and Gordon cuddled up to her almost immediately. She held him close, patting him every so often and continuing to mutter comforting nonsense. Even so, she could feel him trembling quite clearly through his clothes.

The storm seemed to last forever, and it raged around the forest with wild ferocity. At last it seemed to be directly overhead, and when the thunder crashed, it made even the mightiest of the trees tremble and shake. Lightning continued to rip apart the fabric of the sky, adding an unpleasant tingle of electricity and sulphur to the damp air. It grew cooler, downright chilly, in fact, and soon woman and boy were hugging each other just in order to keep warm.

Lauren could hardly credit that she, a grown woman, had got them so completely lost that they might actually have to spend the night out here in the wilds. What had happened to her itinerary, all those organised travel plans?

She didn't know how long it went on for. After a while, she and Gordon both dozed. Sometime much later that night, however, she came awake with a start, but all was quiet and calm. Rain-water dripping off branch-tips and odd, distant animal-sounds — in their own way as unsettling as the storm itself — was all she could hear.

The night dragged on. Gordon slept fitfully in her arms, while Lauren herself tried to doze and thus pass the hours of darkness quicker. At length, she noticed a perceptible lightening of the sky above the leafy canopy sheltering them, and realised with relief that dawn was approaching. Although she felt as exhausted now as she had when the storm had first forced them into the trees, there was something in the promise of daylight that strengthened her resolve.

Gordon stirred sluggishly. The poor mite didn't know where he was at first, as he slowly sat up and knuckled sleep from his eyes.

"Are you all right?" Lauren asked, reaching out to tousle his hair.

He nodded. "Are we lost?" he asked, climbing to his feet and brushing dead leaves from the legs of his jeans.

"We've gone a bit off-course," she replied, keeping her tone light and optimistic to avoid alarming him. "But lost? Never." She paused. "Are you hungry?"

He nodded.

"All I've got are some more sweets, I'm afraid, but they'll have to do until we reach your uncle's farm."

A little while later they gathered their belongings together and set off hand in hand, once again heading for the sunlight filtering greenly through the trees in the distance.

Lauren felt hollow-eyed. Never in a lifetime could she have imagined that their trek to the Wong farm would end in such an adventure, and quite frankly, she felt that both she and Gordon could have done without it. But surely once they were back out on the road, they must inevitably find someone to help them?

Although the storm had brought some temporary relief from the sticky heat, it had evidently been short-lived, and already the morning was warming up.

At last they reached the edge of the forest and emerged into the growing sunlight. But much to Lauren's surprise, they did not find the rutted dirt-track waiting for them. In fact, they could see nothing even remotely resembling a road anywhere.

Her first thought was that the rain had washed out all sign of the track. But she dismissed that notion at once, because it was clearly impossible. No, it soon became obvious that they had set off in the wrong direction, and instead of heading back to the road, they had come out on the far side of the forest.

"Where are we?" Gordon asked, peering up at her. Lauren had turned and was just about to head back the way they had come when she noticed the trees for the first time. They were thick-boled, and wrapped in vines and lianas.

She frowned. Something about them seemed strangely familiar. She felt she had seen them before somewhere, though she knew this could not be so.

She turned again to face the open fields beyond the woods. Ahead of her lay lakes and marshland. A ricefield spread away to the north. Rivers stretched east to west. Hills and valleys lay beyond the farthest of them. And beyond those rose bleak-looking mountains, their peaks shrouded in mist.

It struck her, then, where she had seen all of this before — in her dreams!

A sudden flood of memory came pouring back to engulf her. On her first day in Hong Kong, she had dreamed of this bleak landscape. The second time she had dreamed of it, she had been confronted by an Oriental man she had known she must not trust.

She had not known the identity of

that man at the time, but now she realised with a start that it had been Ricky Lee. As incredible as it seemed, something within her had tried to tell her that he should not be trusted even then, but she had been unable to heed the warning because at that time, she hadn't even known who Ricky Lee was!

She shook her head. No. No, that couldn't be right.

She must be going light-headed. Hunger and lack of sleep were making her imagine —

Before she could ponder the coincidence — for it could hardly be anything else — further, however, they both heard a sudden distant crackling of disturbed undergrowth coming from deep within the confines of the forest.

Gordon made a small, surprised sound in his throat and instinctively reached out for Lauren's hand. The sounds of someone coming through the forest in their direction should not necessarily give cause for alarm, of course, but they were all alone in this remote area, alone and unprotected.

Who was coming towards them through the forest — friend or foe?

She remembered another snippet from her strange dreams then. In the first of them, the man who had come out of the woods had been David Kent. But surely there was no way David could be *here* . . . ?

They saw a movement now, the silhouette of a figure with sunlight and leaf-shadow spilling backward off his shoulders as he approached them. Lauren held onto Gordon, hardly daring to breathe as she tried to discern more details of the newcomer. A moment later she saw that he was tall; athletic; with hair as black as midnight . . .

He came closer, his footsteps loud in the early-morning silence, as disturbed undergrowth crackled beneath his rhythmic tread.

At last the canopy of leaves above him thinned out and sunlight illuminated more details; the tan of his skin; the white flash of his smile; the dark, depthless brown of his eyes . . .

Lauren felt emotion tighten her chest and throat as recognition — a recognition she had been almost afraid to make — finally dawned.

She shook her head in disbelief.

Her voice came out as a whisper filled with wonder.

"David . . . ?"

She could hardly believe the evidence of her suddenly-moist eyes. It *was* David! But what on earth was he doing here?

At last his own eyes came to rest on her smudged face. "*Lauren!*" he said hoarsely. "Thank God!"

He came forward, eating up the ground between them in three long strides, and opened his arms to gather them both to him, woman and child. "God, I must've scoured half of China looking for you two in the last twenty-four hours!"

Lauren was so overcome by emotion that she could hardly speak. She closed her free arm around him, as if he were a figment of her imagination she was reluctant to relinquish. "David . . . " Her voice was husky with suppressed feeling. "David . . . what are *you* doing here?"

As Gordon stood back to allow the grown-ups to hold each other closer, David took Lauren in his arms and pulled her into his warm, strong embrace. "You're not the only one who can take leave from *The Ex-Pat*, you know."

"But . . . " She was so stunned by his sudden appearance that she couldn't even find the words now, and just held him instead.

"How could I let you make this journey alone?" he asked gently. "It was bad enough that I wasn't even able to see you off. So I got to thinking. And on impulse I decided to come after you. I rented a car in Wuzhou and got directions to the Wong farm, but when I got there and you still hadn't arrived, I went back to the city and spoke to the drivers at the bus company. One of them remembered you and young Gordon here from the description I gave him. You'd evidently boarded his bus in Wuzhou, but . . . "

"The bus broke down," Lauren said, taking control of herself again. "When he finally managed to get it working again, he accidentally drove off without us."

"That's the story I was pretty much able to piece together," he said. "So I started out again from Wuzhou first thing this morning, and on impulse took the left fork instead of the right. When I found a sweet-wrapper floating in a puddle at the side of the road, I decided to follow my nose."

"It's a good thing for us that you did," she said gratefully.

"Come on, then," he said. "You'll find the hire car nice and dry after what you two have been through, and once we're back on the right road, we should reach Gordon's uncle's farm in time for breakfast." He reached down and squeezed the little boy's shoulder encouragingly.

"But first," he said, holding Lauren at arm's-length and looking straight into her face, "I want you to take a good long look around you, Lauren. Do you like what you see? No, I didn't think you would. It's remote, bleak, inhospitable, lonely. Oh, it has a certain atmosphere to it. But not the kind of exotic 'magic' you found in Hong Kong, is it?"

She frowned. "I don't understand . . . "

"Do you think there's anything in this wilderness that might influence the way I feel about you?" he asked. "Or the way you feel about me? Any of that 'Hong Kong magic' you spoke of? Of course not. How could romance thrive out here? And yet I'll say it again, Lauren. I love you. I'd love you in the hottest desert or the coldest wasteland. I'd love you and go on loving you, no matter where we were. *Now* will you believe me? And believe what your own heart is telling you?"

232

She looked up into his bronzed, handsome face, saw the earnest sincerity in his dark eyes, and nodded. "Yes, David," she replied softly. "Yes, I'll believe it. And I love you, too. Oh, I love you so much."

"Then don't fight it any more," he said. "We've already wasted so much time."

"Yes," she agreed. "But we have the rest of our lives to make up for it."

He looked down at her, his smile almost brighter than the sun above, and as bright now as her own. "Come on, then," he said again. "First stop, the Wong farm. And then positively the most leisurely return to Hong Kong that you can imagine!"

He slipped one arm about her waist, the other around Gordon's shoulders, and as they began to retrace their steps through the forest to his waiting car, the bleak and inhospitable landscape behind them seemed to lose some of its desolation, and fill instead with promise. Far Eastern promise.

WITH SOMEBODY ELSE
Theresa Charles

Rosamond sets off for Cornwall with Hugo to meet his family, blissfully unaware of the shocks in store for her.

A SUMMER FOR STRANGERS
Claire Hamilton

Because she had lost her job, her flat and she had no money, Tabitha agreed to pose as Adam's future wife although she believed the scheme to be deceitful and cruel.

VILLA OF SINGING WATER
Angela Petron

The disquieting incidents that occurred at the Vatican and the Colosseum did not trouble Jan at first, but then they became increasingly unpleasant and alarming.

DOCTOR NAPIER'S NURSE
Pauline Ash

When cousins Midge and Derry are entered as probationer nurses on the same day but at different hospitals they agree to exchange identities.

A GIRL LIKE JULIE
Louise Ellis

Caroline absolutely adored Hugh Barrington, but then Julie Crane came into their lives. Julie was the kind of girl who attracts men without even trying.

COUNTRY DOCTOR
Paula Lindsay

When Evan Richmond bought a practice in a remote country village he did not realise that a casual encounter would lead to the loss of his heart.

ENCORE
Helga Moray

Craig and Janet realise that their true happiness lies with each other, but it is only under traumatic circumstances that they can be reunited.

NICOLETTE
Ivy Preston

When Grant Alston came back into her life, Nicolette was faced with a dilemma. Should she follow the path of duty or the path of love?

THE GOLDEN PUMA
Margaret Way

Catherine's time was spent looking after her father's Queensland farm. But what life was there without David, who wasn't interested in her?

HOSPITAL BY THE LAKE
Anne Durham

Nurse Marguerite Ingleby was always ready to become personally involved with her patients, to the despair of Brian Field, the Senior Surgical Registrar, who loved her.

VALLEY OF CONFLICT
David Farrell

Isolated in a hostel in the French Alps, Ann Russell sees her fiancé being seduced by a young girl. Then comes the avalanche that imperils their lives.

NURSE'S CHOICE
Peggy Gaddis

A proposal of marriage from the incredibly handsome and wealthy Reagan was enough to upset any girl — and Brooke Martin was no exception.

A DANGEROUS MAN
Anne Goring

Photographer Polly Burton was on safari in Mombasa when she met enigmatic Leon Hammond. But unpredictability was the name of the game where Leon was concerned.

PRECIOUS INHERITANCE
Joan Moules

Karen's new life working for an authoress took her from Sussex to a foreign airstrip and a kidnapping; to a real life adventure as gripping as any in the books she typed.

VISION OF LOVE
Grace Richmond

When Kathy takes over the rundown country kennels she finds Alec Stinton, a local vet, very helpful. But their friendship arouses bitter jealousy and a tragedy seems inevitable.

CRUSADING NURSE
Jane Converse

It was handsome Dr. Corbett who opened Nurse Susan Leighton's eyes and who set her off on a lonely crusade against some powerful enemies and a shattering struggle against the man she loved.

WILD ENCHANTMENT
Christina Green

Rowan's agreeable new boss had a dream of creating a famous perfume using her precious Silverstar, but Rowan's plans were very different.

DESERT ROMANCE
Irene Ord

Sally agrees to take her sister Pam's place as La Chartreuse the dancer, but she finds out there is more to it than dyeing her hair red and looking like her sister.

HEART OF ICE
Marie Sidney

How was January to know that not only would the warmth of the Swiss people thaw out her frozen heart, but that she too would play her part in helping someone to live again?

LUCKY IN LOVE
Margaret Wood

Companion-secretary to wealthy gambler Laura Duxford, who lived in Monaco, seemed to Melanie a fabulous job. Especially as Melanie had already lost her heart to Laura's son, Julian.

NURSE TO PRINCESS JASMINE
Lilian Woodward

Nick's surgeon brother, Tom, performs an operation on an Arabian princess, and she invites Tom, Nick and his fiancé to Omander, where a web of deceit and intrigue closes about them.

THE WAYWARD HEART
Eileen Barry

Disaster-prone Katherine's nickname was "Kate Calamity", but her boss went too far with an outrageous proposal, which because of her latest disaster, she could not refuse.

FOUR WEEKS IN WINTER
Jane Donnelly

Tessa wasn't looking forward to meeting Paul Mellor again — she had made a fool of herself over him once before. But was Orme Jared's solution to her problem likely to be the right one?

SURGERY BY THE SEA
Sheila Douglas

Medical student Meg hadn't really wanted to go and work with a G.P. on the Welsh coast although the job had its compensations. But Owen Roberts was certainly not one of them!

HEAVEN IS HIGH
Anne Hampson

The new heir to the Manor of Marbeck had been found. But it was rather unfortunate that when he arrived unexpectedly he found an uninvited guest, complete with stetson and high boots.

LOVE WILL COME
Sarah Devon

June Baker's boss was not really her idea of her ideal man, but when she went from third typist to boss's secretary overnight she began to change her mind.

ESCAPE TO ROMANCE
Kay Winchester

Oliver and Jean first met on Swale Island. They were both trying to begin their lives afresh, but neither had bargained for complications from the past.

CASTLE IN THE SUN
Cora Mayne

Emma's invalid sister, Kym, needed a warm climate, and Emma jumped at the chance of a job on a Mediterranean island. But Emma soon finds that intrigues and hazards lurk on the sunlit isle.

BEWARE OF LOVE
Kay Winchester

Carol Brampton resumes her nursing career when her family is killed in a car accident. With Dr. Patrick Farrell she begins to pick up the pieces of her life, but is bitterly hurt when insinuations are made about her to Patrick.

DARLING REBEL
Sarah Devon

When Jason Farradale's secretary met with an accident, her glamorous stand-in was quite unable to deal with one problem in particular.

THE PRICE OF PARADISE
Jane Arbor

It was a shock to Fern to meet her estranged husband on an island in the middle of the Indian Ocean, but to discover that her father had engineered it puzzled Fern. What did he hope to achieve?

DOCTOR IN PLASTER
Lisa Cooper

When Dr. Scott Sutcliffe is injured, Nurse Caroline Hurst has to cope with a very demanding private case. But when she realises her exasperating patient has stolen her heart, how can Caroline possibly stay?

A TOUCH OF HONEY
Lucy Gillen

Before she took the job as secretary to author Robert Dean, Cadie had heard how charming he was, but that wasn't her first impression at all.

ROMANTIC LEGACY
Cora Mayne

As kennelmaid to the Armstrongs, Ann Brown, had no idea that she would become the central figure in a web of mystery and intrigue.

THE RELENTLESS TIDE
Jill Murray

Steve Palmer shared Nurse Marie Blane's love of the sea and small boats. Marie's other passion was her step-brother. But when danger threatened who should she turn to — her step-brother or the man who stirred emotions in her heart?

ROMANCE IN NORWAY
Cora Mayne

Nancy Crawford hopes that her visit to Norway will help her to start life again. She certainly finds many surprises there, including unexpected happiness.

UNLOCK MY HEART
Honor Vincent

When Ruth Linton, a young widow with three children, inherits a house in the country, it seems to be the answer to her dreams. But Ruth's problems were only just beginning . . .

SWEET PROMISE
Janet Dailey

Erica had met Rafael in Mexico, where their relationship had been brief but dramatic. Now, over a year later in Texas, she had met him again — and he had the power to wreck her life.

SAFARI ENCOUNTER
Rosemary Carter

Jenny had to accept that she couldn't run her father's game park alone; so she let forceful Joshua Adams virtually take over. But Joshua took over her heart as well!

SHADOW DANCE
Margaret Way

When Carl Danning sent her to interview Richard Kauffman, Alix was far from pleased — but the assignment led her to help Richard repair the situation between him and his ex-wife.

WHITE HIBISCUS
Rosemary Pollock

"A boring English model with dubious morals," was how Count Paul Santana Demajo described Emma. But what about the Count's morals, and who is Marianne?

STARS THROUGH THE MIST
Betty Neels

Secretly in love with Gerard van Doordninck, Deborah should have been thrilled when he asked her to marry him. But he only wanted a wife for practical not romantic reasons.